Only groans and creaks sounded from the old building as it waited for Tom to discover its secret. With a rapidly-beating heart, he approached the staircase...

What is the secret lurking in the ruins of the lonely ghost town in the mountains of British Columbia? Solving the mystery is only one of the challenges facing Tom Austen after he arrives in B.C. with his sidekick, Dietmar Oban, and learns that a young girl has disappeared without a trace. Then a boy is kidnapped, and electrifying events quickly carry Tom to a breathtaking climax deep underground in Cody Caves, where it is forever night...

THE KOOTENAY KIDNAPPER

The Tom and Liz Austen Mysteries
by Eric Wilson

Also available by Eric Wilson
Summer of Discovery

THE
KOOTENAY
KIDNAPPER

Eric Wilson

A TOTEM BOOK
TORONTO

First published 1983
by Collins Publishers
100 Lesmill Road, Don Mills, Ontario

This edition published 1984
by TOTEM BOOKS
a division of Collins Publishers

Canadian Cataloguing in Publication Data
Wilson, Eric.
    The Kootenay kidnapper

ISBN 0-00-222842-4

I. Title.

PS8595.I4793K66 1984   jC813'.54   C84-098551-7
PZ7.W55Ko 1984

Printed in Canada

Nelson is, of course, a real city in British Columbia, but all the characters in this book are fictitious and any resemblance to real people is entirely coincidental.

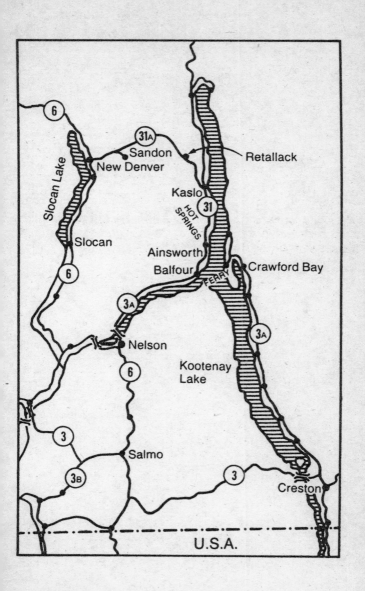

1

WHERE IS TIPPI ALLEN?

Below these words was a picture of Tippi's smiling face. Her eyes were large and brown, and she held a doll as she looked innocently from the poster. She was just eight years old, and had been missing for a week.

Tom Austen shook his head, feeling sad for Tippi. Local people had talked about nothing else since she had disappeared, just when Tom arrived on holiday in Nelson, a small city in the mountains of southeastern British Columbia.

A boy of ten stopped at the poster. "I know Tippi," he said to Tom, who was sitting on a bench inside Nelson's Chahko-Mika Mall. "She goes to Hume School with me."

"Are all the kids upset?"

"School's out for the summer, but we got called back for a special meeting in the gym. The principal told us how to protect ourselves against kidnappers. We're not supposed to talk to strangers."

Tom smiled. "Aren't I a stranger?"

"That's different! You're just a kid. Anyway, I can look after myself. Tippi made a mistake, taking the shortcut to the mall along the railway tracks, but I'm not that dumb."

Shoppers passed in the mall, some talking to their children, others looking in the store windows. Did one of them secretly know the truth about Tippi?

"What's your name?" Tom asked the boy.

"Chuck Cohen."

"Listen, Chuck, do you . . ."

Tom's question was interrupted by the approach of a man who seemed highly excited. Wearing a security guard uniform and peaked cap, he was snapping the fingers of both hands as he stopped at the bench.

"Either of you know Tippi Allen?"

"Sure," Chuck replied.

"Listen, son, we've just had a tremendous break in the case. There's every chance that Tippi is going to be found alive, but we need your help."

"That's wonderful! What can I do?"

"Just come with me."

Chuck jumped up from the bench, but Tom grabbed his arm. "Hold it," he said, then looked at the man.

2

"Shouldn't you show Chuck some identification?"

The man's fingers stopped snapping, and suddenly Tom was frightened. There was no way to see the man's eyes, because they were hidden behind sunglasses, but he sensed intense hostility. "What's your name?"

"Uh, I'm ... Tom Austen."

"Do you know Tippi, Tom?"

"No, but ..."

"Then you shouldn't get involved." The man started walking away with Chuck, then stopped. Taking out his wallet, he flipped it open, A gold badge flashed. "Here's my ID Tom, since you don't trust me."

Tom blushed, and he cursed himself for being one of those redheads whose faces reveal their secret thoughts. Feeling stupid, he dropped his eyes to the carpet and studied the design, trying to believe he'd just seen a genuine ID, and Chuck was really on his way to save Tippi. From the nearby Wizard's Castle came the blipping of video games and the laughter of teenagers, enjoying their Friday night at the mall. Why wasn't he?

Tom wandered in to watch a game of *Phantom II*, but his heart thumped painfully when he thought about Chuck. If something happened to him, it would be Tom's fault. Turning, he forced a path through the shoppers and ran toward the exit door and out into the black night.

A warm summer wind came off the nearby lake, blowing gently on Tom's face. Mercury-vapour lights hissed from high above the parking lot, shining on rows of cars and pickup trucks. Where was Chuck? Tom took a few steps in one direction, stopped, and looked around helplessly. A sick panic wrenched his stomach.

Tom hurried toward a row of taxis, hoping one of the drivers had seen Chuck leaving with the security guard. But then he got a break. For a brief moment a cigarette lighter flared inside a parked car, and Tom recognized the peaked cap and sunglasses of the security guard.

Sunglasses at night? As he approached the car, Tom's pulse was beating so strongly that he could feel each stroke. "Excuse me," he said, knocking on the window. "May I speak to Chuck?"

The man rolled down the glass. "You again?"

Tom looked at Chuck. "I think you should get out of this car."

Ignoring Tom, the boy stared straight ahead. Then, with a shaking hand, he slowly raised a bottle of pop to his lips. Some of the dark liquid spilled down his chin as he swallowed.

"Chuck, please! Get out of this car."

The driver smiled, his white teeth gleaming in the dark. "Get outta here, Tom!" He reached for the gearshift, and the car rolled smoothly away.

Tom scribbled down the car's licence number, and the name of a car rental company he'd seen on the bumper, then ran toward a taxi.

"Ma'am!" he shouted to the driver, a middle-aged woman who was reading the *Nelson Daily News*. "You've got to help me. A kid's in a lot of trouble."

"What's the problem?"

"That car," Tom said, pointing at a pair of red taillights leaving a distant exit, "Please, just follow it, and I'll explain."

4

"Are you paying for this trip?"

"Sure, if you want." Tom grabbed the nearest door handle, and tumbled into the back seat. "Don't lose them!"

Gunning the motor, the woman laughed. "What is this, the Late Show? I've always dreamed Paul Newman would jump into my cab and shout *follow that car!* but this is ridiculous."

Despite her amusement, the driver sensed Tom's urgency and they drove quickly out of the parking lot. Tom leaned forward, trying to spot the security guard's car as they approached an intersection.

"There it is! Turning left at those traffic lights."

Just after the taxi banged over some railway tracks, the traffic lights changed and the driver was forced to stop. "Bad luck. But you can tell me what's happening while we wait for the green."

As quickly as possible, Tom explained his suspicions. "I'm sure he's not a real security guard. He just used that fake badge and uniform as a disguise, so Chuck would trust him. There were probably drugs in that drink he gave Chuck. He was totally zombied. *The light's green!*"

With a scream of rubber, the taxi leapt away from the corner. "I have my doubts," the driver said, her hands tight on the wheel, "but I'm not taking any chances. Not after poor Tippi."

"Did you know her?"

"Tippi and my son played on the same soccer team."

"There's the car! What should we do?"

"Leave it to me." Pulling up close, the woman flashed the taxi's high beams. The security guard

5

looked in his rear-view mirror, then gestured with his hand. Again the taxi lights flashed, and the driver leaned on the horn. "Pull over, buddy, or I'll get mean."

The security guard twisted his wheel, and the car turned into a side street. After travelling a short distance, it stopped. The taxi stopped too, keeping well away. "We'll watch from here for a minute, in case he takes off."

The security guard stepped calmly out of his car. He adjusted his peaked cap, then stood waiting, smoking a cigarette.

"Let's talk to him," the woman said, getting out. She walked forward fearlessly, but Tom's mouth was dry, and his eyes flicked over the security guard, looking for signs of a hidden weapon.

"Is there a problem?" the man asked, smiling.

"I hope not," she replied. "This young man thinks you've abducted a boy against his will."

The security guard's laugh was low and rich. He seemed totally relaxed, and the blush crept back across Tom's face. What if he'd made a terrible mistake?

"Look," he said desperately, "can we talk to Chuck, just for a minute?"

"Certainly!" The man waved a hand toward his car. "Go right ahead."

The woman frowned at Tom, and he swallowed unhappily. It looked as though he had blundered. But, when they reached the car, Chuck was lying on the front seat, unable to speak. His eyes had the dull gleam of marbles, and the sweat on his face was cold to Tom's touch.

"You were right," the driver exclaimed. "This boy's in a bad way."

Straightening up, she looked for the security guard. For a moment he couldn't be seen, then Tom pointed toward the taxi's headlights. The security guard came out of the dazzling light, and approached them.

"All I wanna do," he said in his deep voice, "is get that boy to the hospital."

"What *I* want," the woman said angrily, "is to find out what's happening. Why's that boy so sick?"

The man held up his hand. "The hospital first, the talk after. Okay? Follow me in your taxi."

She nodded, and ran back to her car. Feeling totally confused, and very worried about Chuck, Tom hurried to the passenger door and got inside. But the car was dead. The ignition wires of the car, slashed and useless, dangled from under the dashboard; the radio microphone had also been cut away.

Horrified, Tom looked down the street. In the distance, the red tail-lights of the security guard's car disappeared into the night.

2

"Some maniac has declared war on our kids."

The man who said this was called Tattoo. He had wild shaggy hair, a good-looking face turning pudgy, and muscular arms which showed tattoos of a skull and crossbones, an easy rider, and a cobra wrapped around and around his brown and hairy arm.

"If the cops don't stop that creep, I will."

The woman sitting next to Tattoo murmured, "Take it easy, sugar." Moving closer, she rested her head against his shoulder.

"Nobody's safe," Tattoo said. "One of *your* kids could be next, Shirleen."

"Don't say that, sugar. You're scaring us, and this is supposed to be a fun trip." She turned, and smiled at the other people jammed into the old car. "Everyone happy?"

"You bet," Tom replied, although truthfully he was still shaky about last night's abduction of Chuck Cohen. The boy had disappeared, along with the man who'd pretended to be a security guard. Nelson was in turmoil, and extra police were pouring in to help track the kidnapper.

Beside Tom was Dietmar Oban, whom he'd known for years, and Theolonius P. Judd, also known as the Maestro. This tall and handsome man, who wore an immaculate suit with white shirt and tie despite the heat, was Dietmar's uncle and had flown the boys from Winnipeg as his guests. The Maestro claimed to be a master at making money, and wanted to explore the Kootenays for new financial opportunities.

Also squeezed into the car were Shirleen's grandmother, a fragile, grey-haired woman known as Great Granny, and a teen-ager, Brandi, who was Shirleen's daughter. Tom was constantly aware of Brandi, stealing glances at her large dark eyes, or watching as she ran slim fingers through her luxurious hair. Tattoo, who was laid off from his job in the woods, was taking them to see a logger sports event. Like the Maestro and the boys, Tattoo rented a room at *Shirleen's Place*, the guest house in Nelson which Shirleen ran with the aid of her grandmother and Brandi. The Maestro explained that renting rooms at a guest house was the best way to meet local people.

Tom tried to concentrate on the beauty of the passing scene. The car was travelling along the northern lakeshore; beyond the sparkle of waves leaping behind a speedboat lay the mountains, still deeply shadowed except for valleys, where morning sunshine touched thick forests of evergreens.

"Hey, Maestro," Tattoo said, "wait till you see the Glass House. It was built by a funeral director, using left-over embalming fluid bottles. Some people say it's haunted by his old customers."

Dietmar's uncle laughed. "How atrocious, and how very perfect. That man knew how to make a dollar."

"Speaking of glass," Dietmar said, "do you know why Tom Austen climbed the glass wall? To see what was on the other side."

Brandi giggled, and a pain stabbed through Tom. "Know how to keep a turkey in suspense, Oban?"

"Nope."

"I'll tell you next week."

Brandi rewarded this brilliance with a faint smile. Feeling rotten, Tom stared out at a sternwheeler deckhouse, stranded on a hillside. Empty windows looked toward the lake where the boat had once carried gold and silver, and the miners who opened up the area.

"The remains of the *S.S. Nasookin*," Great Granny said grimly. "The meals I had on that steamer! Kootenay Strawberries on bone china, served up on a white tablecloth while we kept watch for moose swimming out to gore the boat."

"How'd they get strawberries into the wilderness?"

Shirleen smiled. "Don't let my Grandma fool you, Tom. Kootenay Strawberries were beans, plain and simple."

10

"But the food *was* good, and so were the times. The boats used to race down the lake, black smoke and sparks belching, the paddlewheels pounding the water. Marvellous! The fastest steamer was awarded a set of antlers, to lash to the pilot house."

"Did you work on a paddlewheeler?"

"No chance. I was a dancing girl."

Shirleen frowned. "Must you mention that, Grandmother? I tell people you were a pioneer."

"Then those people must think I'm six feet under, pushing up daisies. I'm not ashamed because I entertained the miners. They had a tough life. I remember Tommy Gynt, what a man he was. Tommy used to crimp blasting caps in his teeth, until one of them blew off his head."

Shirleen sighed unhappily, but Brandi laughed. "Your boy-friends were real macho, Great Granny. I wish mine were tougher."

Remembering the isometric exercises he'd been using to build his muscles, Tom put his hands together and pressed hard. Then he flexed his biceps, wondering how they'd look with a biker or a skull etched deep into the skin.

Reaching Balfour, they joined a line of cars waiting to cross the lake by ferry. Soon the ferry swept dramatically into view, white water foaming up from its low, flat bow. Tourists lined the railing, waving and aiming cameras as the vessel slid slowly into its berth. Cars and vans rolled off, followed by two women on a motorcycle with a Washington licence plate.

"My sister Liz would flip," Tom said, grinning. "Those women aren't wearing helmets, and that's against the law here in B.C."

As soon as they were on board the ferry, Tom went

11

to the railing. A cooling wind rippled the lake. Then the breeze changed direction, scattering sunshine, making the surface dance with beauty; most of the lake was deep and black, but along the shore the water was a pale green. Nearby were both expensive sailboats and small outboards, engines sputtering as they warmed up before heading out to fish the vast waters of Kootenay Lake.

"Where'd this area get its name?" Tom asked Tattoo, as the man joined him.

"Kootenay is an Indian word, meaning 'water people.' This lake is well known for the Kokanee salmon, which got trapped here after the ice age and couldn't return to the Pacific. Good eating, man."

Tattoo slapped his round belly, then grinned and squeezed Tom's neck with a strong hand. Tom returned his smile, liking the man even though his fast driving along the twisting North Shore Road had been hair-raising.

"What are logger sports, Tattoo?"

"Half of B.C. is forest, Tom, so logging's a big industry. The old-time loggers used to test each other, racing up trees or tossing axes at a bull's-eye. Now we compete with power saws, cutting up giant logs."

"What's your favourite event?"

"The log rolling. Two big men in their spiked boots, spinning a log back and forth, trying to throw each other into the water."

"Will you be competing?"

Tattoo hooted. "I'm getting too old."

The ferry left its berth, heading for open waters. Tom's T-shirt blew in the wind, and he heard the pleasant sound of waves leaping away from the hull as he waved to a man whose fishing line trailed from his boat down into the cold, dark water.

"This is the good life, Tom. Except for that plane, I'd feel happy."

Tom looked up at the small Piper, which was buzzing slowly along the shoreline, just above the water. "What about it?"

"That's an RCMP plane. The police are searching for the bodies of those kids."

Sickness swept through Tom like a wave. He gripped the railing, staring at the plane until it was gone. How could someone who lived in all this beauty hurt kids? Tears stung his eyes, but he squeezed them back. If only he could help!

"*I* let him get away, Tattoo. I should have yelled at someone in the mall to grab him."

"Hey, buddy, just relax. Say, aren't those Purcells something?"

The far shore of Kootenay Lake was solid mountains. Forest grew up their sides, then gave way to grey rock and the snow-covered jagged summits which cut the sky. To the south, the Purcell Mountains stretched into the distance, each a paler shade of blue until they were lost in the heat-haze.

"Somewhere near Crawford Bay is the Nelson Nugget. It's worth millions of dollars, but no one can find it."

"The Maestro could."

"I told him about it. Unfortunately the nugget's under 120 metres of water. That depth can give a diver the bends."

"How'd it get down there?"

"Prospectors found the huge chunk of solid gold in

13

1892. They were lowering it down a rocky cliff into a rowboat when their rope broke. The gold smashed through the boat and sank to the bottom."

"What a waste! If I could find that nugget, I'd retire from school and hire Dietmar as my slave-boy. He could lace my Nikes and brush my teeth."

"How disgusting," Tattoo said, laughing. "By the way, your buddy seems to like Brandi a lot."

Tattoo looked toward the stern, where Dietmar was pointing his camera at the gorgeous Brandi. The wind, which was lifting and blowing and caressing her black hair, rippled the words *Here comes trouble* on her T-shirt; other passengers watched with interest as Dietmar shot Brandi from different angles.

"Pure Hollywood," Tom muttered as Dietmar crawled onto a lifeboat with his camera. "What a loser!"

"Move in, man. Give him some competition."

"Forget it. Brandi means nothing to me."

Hands in his pockets, whistling feebly, Tom returned to the car. Shortly after, the ferry bumped gently into the landing. To Tom's surprise, Tattoo ignored the officer in charge and drove off the ferry before his turn. As the officer shouted, Tattoo grinned.

Soon they reached Crawford Bay. After parking on the grass in someone's front yard, Tattoo led them to a park rapidly filling with spectators. From a small arena came the pounding of metal against wood as loggers warmed up. Sunshine flashed from an axe blade as a huge man heaved it end-over-end toward the butt end of a log, marked with a bull's-eye. It hit with a *chunk* that sounded across the park.

Dietmar grinned. "It's the mad axeman! Keep clear

of him, Austen. He may want to part your hair."

"Or make me part with my head. But I need it, to keep may ears separated."

The Maestro clucked his tongue. "Why aren't they selling authentic Logger Sports T-shirts? Balloons, pencils, rulers, coffee mugs! These people aren't thinking money; I could turn this into another Calgary Stampede!"

Tom sniffed the mountain air; mingled with its clean fragrance was the smell of food. He was soon sitting at a picnic table with a hot dog buried under mustard, ketchup, relish and home-made pickles. Feeling good, he looked up at the shady forests on the mountains, and the perfect blue of the sky.

"I wish we could take this place home," he said, as the Maestro and Dietmar sat down with their hamburgers.

The Maestro chewed vigorously. "I'd like to take home the recipe for these pickles."

A man passed wearing a straw cowboy hat, checked shirt, jeans and cowboy boots; a camera with a huge black lens bounced against his stomach. Beside the man was a teen-age girl in a half-shirt, shorts and knee-socks. Tom smiled at her, then his face froze as Brandi approached. Trying to appear nonchalant, he reached for a cob of corn.

"What's wrong, Tom, are you ignoring me?" Brandi sat down beside him. "I thought you'd take my picture on the ferry."

"Joe Hollywood got enough to fill three albums. I'll look at his." The deep-yellow cob glistened as Tom lifted it to his teeth; sweet and succulent, its taste enriched by butter and salt, the corn was soon gone.

"I need my camera for other things."

Dietmar snorted. "Austen is into his Great Detective routine. Pictures of all suspects, notes on their movements. Watch out, Brandi, or he'll finger you for the kidnappings."

Brandi looked straight at Tom, and his heart skipped. "Is it true you've actually helped solve some crimes?"

Tom shrugged. "A couple."

"Would you tell me about them some time?"

"Sure!"

Dietmar's eyes were flickering between Brandi and Tom. "Austen's just been lucky in the past. This time he'll probably get himself kidnapped."

"No chance."

"Don't bet on it, meatball."

A loudspeaker announced the approach of the parade to open the festivities. Brandi and Dietmar hurried off, but Tom remained behind, drinking lemonade as he wondered who the kidnapper could be. A shadow fell across the table, and he looked up at a boy his own age with blond hair, blue eyes and a deep tan.

"Who's that beauty you were with?"

"Just someone," Tom mumbled, getting up to take his paper plate to a litter bin. "Her name's Brandi Sokoloski. Why?"

"I'd like to meet her." The boy held out a strong hand. "I'm Simon Sikula. My team's down from Tumbler Ridge for the midsummer hockey tournament in Nelson. You playing, too?"

"No, but I'd sure like to see some games."

"Our first is tomorrow at noon. How about cheering us on?"

Tom nodded, smiling. "Maybe I'll bring Brandi. Or would she be too distracting?"

"With her there, I'll play like a demon possessed."

At the stands in the arena the pair watched the parade, which ended with the Crawford Bay Elementary School Marching Kazoo Band playing *The Saints*. Close by sat the Maestro, Dietmar and Brandi, who immediately started flirting with Simon in a way that made Tom feel uncomfortable, but there was no sign of the others. Finally Tom spotted Tattoo in the shade of a distant fence, talking to some competitors.

Huge logs waited in the middle of the arena for the first event, the power-saw bucking. After the announcer explained the contest the men raced to the logs. The air filled with the high-pitched roar of their powerful saws, and wood chips flew as the steel cut deep. Immediately Tom knew the winner would be a heavily-muscled logger who leaned low over his saw, forcing it rapidly down. With a final screaming *rnnnnnnnn!* from his engine, a slice of log like a big pizza fell to the ground.

Blue exhaust smoke drifted over the stands, making Tom squint, followed by the smell of freshly-cut wood. Tattoo came forward to hold up the winner's arm while the crowd applauded.

Then a strange thing happened.

As he looked at the crowd Tattoo was grinning hugely, almost as if he had won the contest. His eyes found Tom and winked, then they moved on. Suddenly, shock crossed Tattoo's face. After staring into the crowd for a full minute, he turned away.

What had upset Tattoo? He had been looking in the direction of Brandi and Simon, who were leaning together having a very intense discussion, but that didn't explain anything to Tom.

Puzzled, he looked across the arena at Tattoo, wondering what his secret was.

3

Shortly after, the group left the logger sports.

Shirleen fetched them from the stands, and they found Tattoo waiting at the car. Immediately he quarrelled with Brandi when she complained about having to leave, and tension was thick until they reached the Glass House and they were able to laugh about living behind walls of embalming-fluid bottles.

Tattoo, however, didn't join in the fun.

Emotion hung over the man like a cloud. He said nothing as the drive continued, then rushed them through the Creston Wildlife Sanctuary even though he'd raved about it for days.

The worst was yet to come. Heading toward the Skyway, the highway over the mountains to Salmo, they rounded a bend and saw police officers waiting. Tattoo swore, and for a moment it seemed he might refuse to pull over. When he did, the officers were very polite, explaining the roadblock was part of the search for the missing children, but Tattoo was so rude that Tom's face burned with embarrassment.

When they were moving again, the Maestro made an effort to be cheerful. "Know how I'd make money from that wildlife sanctuary? I'd set up a bird-food restaurant."

Great Granny laughed. "People wouldn't pay to eat bird seed."

"You misunderstand, dear lady. I'd feed birds to humans. Duck à l'orange, roast heron, osprey in plum sauce. The customer sits at the restaurant window, picks the bird he wants, then watches the waiter bag it, right in the wild."

Tom smiled. Outside his window evening sunshine streamed across a richly forested valley and turned the mountain peaks a smoky blue. A swift river, swirling among huge boulders, reflected the golden light of the sun.

"Look at that forest ranger's post across the valley," Dietmar said. "There's a lonely job for you. I wonder what they do for fun? There can't be any TV to watch."

"If I owned that post," said the Maestro, "I'd rent it to a hermit, then make extra by charging the government when my hermit spotted a forest fire."

Tattoo turned to him. "You looking for a hermit to

rent that place? Try me. Lately I feel like dropping out
of life."

The next day, Tom sat with Brandi in the stands at the
hockey rink. Dietmar, not wanting them to be alone,
had tagged along.

"Get some wood on it!" he yelled at Simon. "You
play like an old man!"

Tom laughed. "Your jealousy is showing, Oban.
Simon's the best one out there."

Brandi nodded. "I only wish he used his muscles
more. He should be creaming those Nelson players
into the boards."

"They haven't done anything."

"So what? You've got to rough them up in advance,
so they're scared. That's what hockey's all about."

She jumped to her feet as Simon took a pass and cut
in over the blue line. He faked a slapshot, then slid the
puck to a second Tumbler Ridge player whose shot
was low and hard. At the last second the Nelson
goalie's skate came out of nowhere to block the puck;
Simon picked up the rebound right in front, but
somehow the goalie sprawled to make a second great
save.

"Fantastic hockey," Tom said, as the whistle blew
and the happy Nelson players pounded the goalie's
pads with their sticks. "I'm enjoying this."

"I'm not." Brandi beckoned to Simon as he skated
to his team's bench, and fresh troops poured onto the
ice. "Simon!" she shouted. "Lay into them. Take the
body!"

Simon smiled, then slumped down on the bench and grabbed a water bottle. Sweat poured down his face as he listened to his coach abuse the team for their mistakes. The man didn't look right for hockey, with his meaty face under a pork-pie hat and his beer belly bulging over a cowboy belt, but he seemed to care passionately. Tension marked his eyes, and he was hoarse from shouting.

"He bothers me," Tom said. "He's so lippy to his players."

"That's the right attitude," Brandi replied. "His team's going to win. Nelson hasn't got a chance. Kendall Steele isn't even involved, so why should his team care?"

The Nelson coach, Kendall Steele, stood quietly behind his team's bench, hands in the pockets of his carefully-tailored suit as he spoke to the team's manager. There was a roar from the stands, and the men looked toward the Tumbler Ridge goal, where a defenceman was smashing his stick against the ice, and the goalie knelt in shame, head hanging.

"Nelson scored!" Tom shouted above the roaring crowd. "Your theory's full of holes, Brandi."

She smiled. "It's not over yet. You'll see, Tom. This is a battle of coaching styles, and my money's on that guy Burton Donco from Tumbler Ridge."

At the Nelson bench the jubilant players were receiving brief pats on the back from Kendall Steele, while Tumbler Ridge was being bitterly attacked by red-faced Burton Donco. Tom shook his head, and leaned back to enjoy his Coke.

The rink was a colourful scene, with bright lights shining on the players' plastic helmets and their vivid uniforms. The air was cold and fresh, the gleaming ice hissed with the metallic sound of skates, and the spectators' faces were alive with excitement.

"I may stay here all day," Tom said.

Dietmar snorted. "What about the kidnapper? Aren't you going after him?"

"No way. I wouldn't tangle with someone that dangerous. The police will get him."

Brandi sighed. "I hope it's soon. I'm freaked."

"You don't have to worry," Dietmar said. "You're not the right age."

"How do you know? Maybe he's taken older kids we haven't heard about. Some people from my school are listed as runaways, but who knows for sure? Maybe some creep got them."

"Those things don't happen."

"Oh yes they do. Haven't you heard of that low-grade jerk who murdered all those kids at the coast? He cruised around, picking up hitchers or kids at bus stops, flashing a fancy business card and offering work. They trusted him, just because he looked like a businessman."

"Why didn't they jump out of his car?"

"Because he gave them doped pop, or capsules he called pep pills which were actually knock-out drops. If you get in a guy's car, and he wants to kill you, there's no escape."

"It couldn't happen to me."

Brandi's soft hair brushed Tom as she leaned to shake Dietmar's hand. "It's been nice knowing you."

"Give it up, Brandi. You can't scare me."

But he did look worried. Tom was upset, too, but got back into the excitement when Tumbler Ridge tied the score and then pressed hard as Nelson began to tire. With a minute to go, a Tumbler Ridge player broke in fast, faked a shot, then dropped the puck to Simon and cut across the goal. For a split second the goalie's vision was blocked, and Simon blasted a low shot that bulged the net.

Delirious with joy, the Tumbler Ridge players surrounded Simon. Brandi was all smiles as she turned to Tom. "I should have bet money. My coach wins!"

"You're right, Brandi," Tom said, looking in disappointment at Kendall Steele. The Nelson coach remained absolutely still during the dying seconds of the game as his team fought unsuccessfully to tie the score. When the game was over he calmly lit a cigarette, straightened his suit coat, and walked away from the bench.

Burton Donco was the exact opposite, pounding his players on the back and squeezing them in bear hugs. Tom got past him to congratulate Simon, arranged to meet the next day, and headed for the exit. He felt like being on his own, even though it meant giving Dietmar time alone with Brandi.

Outside the rink the sun blasted down, and he hurried to a shady street. As he walked, Tom stared at Nelson's classic old houses with their elaborate gingerbread decorations, conical roofs and bay windows filled with green plants. He hadn't seen houses like these since visiting Lunenburg.

"Hey, kid."

Tom turned, and saw a woman at the wheel of a car. Beside her, a man was studying a map of Nelson.

"Come here, please," the woman said. "We need help."

Somewhere inside Tom a voice warned him to keep his distance. Nearby houses looked empty, and there was no one else walking who could help. There were no stores or service stations where he could run. No taxi drivers to radio the police.

"We're lost," the woman said. "Where's City Hall?" Tom gave the directions, but nervousness made him mumble and the woman frowned. "I can't hear you. Come closer, will you?"

Tom stayed where he was, and repeated the directions in a louder voice. His eyes scanned the street, looking for a trash can he could knock over if he needed to make noise to attract attention. His mouth was suddenly very dry.

The man threw the map into the back seat, then got out and leaned across the car, looking at Tom. "Listen, son, we're both journalists," he said in a patient voice. "There's a press conference at City Hall about the missing kids, and we're late for it. We could lose our jobs if we mess up." He paused, smiling. "Would you do us a big favour?"

"What is it?"

"Jump in the car, and show us the way. We'll give you some money to grab a taxi home."

Tom shook his head. "I'd better not."

Suddenly the man slammed his hand down on the car. "What are you, some kind of wimp?" he shouted. "This is important!' Here's my press pass, with my picture. Don't you believe we're journalists?"

Tom looked down the street. At the far end was a sign, showing the way to the hospital. He could get help there, or at a fire hall. Keeping his eye on the car, he began walking.

"Come back here!" the man yelled. At the same moment, the woman gunned the car's engine. Tom's heart jumped, and he took off running.

He didn't stop until he reached the hospital.

4

The next morning, Tom told Simon about the journalists.

"As it turned out, they were genuine. I saw them on TV, asking questions at the press conference. But I'm glad I didn't take a chance."

"Me too," Simon said. "Obviously they found City Hall without your help."

"They made me feel so guilty."

"Anyone's allowed to say no. Other adults would congratulate you for protecting your life."

"Well," Tom said, smiling, "it's sure nice to be alive on a morning like this."

The boys sat on the rocky shore, looking across the lake at the sunshine which touched the roofs of the white houses of Nelson. Standing watch over the city was a mountain with a forest climbing all the way to its single peak. Above the mountain was the pale blue of the sky, misted with trailing clouds.

The squeaky cry of a bird sounded over the water, and the lake made low, liquid sounds as it washed gently around the big boulders where Tom and Simon sat. For a long time they were silent, until their thoughts were disturbed by a car whooshing past on the nearby North Shore Road.

"Your team's good, Simon. I think you'll win the tournament."

"If we don't, Burton Donco will take us apart. He's the worst coach I've ever had."

"I wasn't too impressed, but Brandi said his attitude was right."

"All that screaming? I hate it. You should hear him swearing in the dressing room; it's really gross. I may quit hockey."

"That's nuts, Simon. You're good enough to play pro hockey."

"Well, maybe I'll stick it out. Other coaches are pretty good. Ours just isn't playing with a full deck."

Tom looked down at the tiny brown fish which played under the crystal surface of the lake, enjoying the way they moved to a position, held it for long seconds, then powered away. A dragonfly came darting across the water, its long tubular body resembling a military transport helicopter.

"Ever been in a helicopter, Simon?"

"That's my best memory of Dad. When I was four, he paid a helicopter pilot to take us up. We did all these crazy headstands and things. It was terrifying, and I loved it."

"Is your father dead?"

Simon was silent, then shook his head. "No, but he might as well be. A year ago he pulled out, and Mom's never heard a word. Finally we moved to Tumbler Ridge so she could find work."

"Are you angry with your dad?"

"Wouldn't you be? Sometimes I hear Mom crying, and I want to find Dad and beat on him. But I've got his picture on my wall, and I love him when I look at that picture. He was a great dad, the best."

"Maybe he'll come back."

"I won't hold my breath." Simon looked up at the tall pines, their branches bristling with long green spikes. "Know what a crowbar is?"

"A work tool."

"Wrong. It's a place where blackbirds go for a drink."

"When you pour scalding water down a rabbit hole, what do you get?"

"Give up."

"Hot cross bunnies."

They both laughed, then fell into a long silence which was disturbed only by the occasional passing car, and once by a jogger whose shoes made a *flip-flop, flip-flop* sound as she passed. Tom studied the black and brown markings of a spider which waited patiently for a victim to blunder into its silky web, then watched a breeze move back and forth on the lake, breaking the surface into thousands of sparkling diamonds.

"What do you think of Brandi?"

Simon grinned. "You fond of her?"

"I guess so," Tom said, feeling suddenly shy. "I don't know for sure. She's so good to look at, but I can't think of anything to talk to her about."

"That's not your fault. What has she asked about you?"

"Not much. She seemed interested because I've solved some crimes, but she forgot to get the details. We're meeting at the Big Tee for cheeseburgers, so maybe she'll ask then."

"And maybe she won't." Simon ran a hand through his blond hair. "Ever notice how people stare at little girls who are super pretty? Kids like that grow up thinking they don't have to make an effort. They just stand around, and everyone goes gaga over them. Life's too easy, so they're boring people."

"My sister Liz is really pretty, and she isn't boring."

"Introduce me!" Simon said, smiling. "Meanwhile, I'll continue to have girlfriends who look like ordinary people and are fun to be with."

A fly landed on Tom's hand, so gently that he hardly noticed. At the same moment, a footstep sounded softly behind him. Turning, Tom saw an old man with white hair, shaggy eyebrows hanging over his eyes, and a thick white moustache.

"Excuse me, boys." The man came closer, leaning on a cane of polished hardwood. "Have you seen a puppy around here?"

"No," Simon said, shaking his head. "Is it lost?"

"That's right." The man lifted his cane with a hand that trembled, and pointed along the road. "I live just around that corner. My grandchildren are staying for the summer. The little girl brought her puppy, and I let it get out of the garden. It was my fault: I just forgot and left the gate open, and I'm very upset. The little girl will be heartbroken."

Tom stood up, and looked at the curving road. He remembered how fast Tattoo had driven it, wheels screaming around the corners. A lost and frightened puppy wouldn't have a chance.

"Can we help find it?"

"Wonderful!" The old man clicked his tongue. "Never again will I criticize today's youth! It's so good of you to help, and I promise a generous reward."

As he turned toward the road, Simon winked at Tom. "We'll do our best, sir. What's the puppy's name?"

There was a pause, then the man shook his head. "Do you know, I can't remember. Fluffy maybe, or Spot? My memory's going."

After they'd searched a short section of the road, the man pointed his cane at some woods. "Do you think the puppy might be hiding in there, boys?"

"Could be," Tom replied. "Let's try."

Evergreens closed around them, smelling sweet, and the outside world was cut off as they walked. The sun's rays poured down in bright shafts, lighting up the trees in radiant green; spongy ground cushioned their feet. A path ran through the forest, long and crooked, pointing the way into darkness.

Tom shivered. For the first time, he noticed the birds had fallen silent. This would be a perfect place for a puppy to hide, crouching under a low bush until the little girl came to find it, but it would have to be on its guard. Enemies might be hiding, waiting to strike.

Tom walked slowly forward, wondering how they'd ever find a puppy in all these shadows, and then his stomach clenched. Above his head, at the end of a thin branch, was a death's head.

Tom moved closer, and realized he was looking at a hornet's nest, dark and eerie, its base punched with a black hole like an ugly, shrieking mouth. He stared at it, aware of fear rushing through his body. Why was Simon being so quiet?

Tom turned, and his horrified hand flew up to his mouth.

Simon and the old man were locked in a silent struggle. The man had grabbed Simon from behind, had twisted an arm around his throat, and was squeezing so hard that Simon's face had turned purple.

"Don't move!" the man ordered Tom. "Get down."

Tom dropped to his knees. His entire body was trembling violently. Simon's face went darker, then he collapsed. The man tried to stop Simon from dropping to the ground, then bent over his body.

Tom's hand was touching loose dirt. With sudden energy he scooped some up and leapt toward the man, throwing the dirt into his face. As the man cried out, and clawed at his eyes, Tom made a break for the road. He had to stop a car, get help.

"Come back!"

Tom ran faster, not believing they had gone so deep into the woods. They'd been fools! He heard the sound of feet in pursuit. His heart filled his chest, and hot breath burned his throat. Run!

Bursting from the woods, Tom dashed onto the road. His eyes searched for cars, but nothing moved in the burning sunshine. Noise came from the woods, then the man ran out. The white hair on his head was crooked — obviously a wig — and now Tom noticed he wore scuffed cowboy boots. How many old men wear cowboy boots? Tom cursed himself for being so easily tricked.

For a moment the man rubbed at his eyes, still half-blinded by the dirt. Tom looked up and down the empty road for cars, then started to run. Again the feet came after him, the swift feet of a man powerful enough to choke the life out of Simon. Tom put down his head, tried to find energy, but he knew the man was getting closer.

He looked up, and suddenly hope was straight ahead.

On a telephone pole, red and shining, waiting for his hand.

Somehow he must reach it. The feet were so close now that Tom could hear the man's harsh breathing.

He ran, swiftly, desperately.

He reached out.

His hand clutched the red fire alarm, and he pulled. Then he fell to his knees, exhausted, unable to do anything more, waiting for the hands of the man.

But no hands touched him. Instead there was a single angry swear word, followed by the sound of feet; the man was running away before help could come to Tom. He remained kneeling, filling his burning lungs with air, until he heard the sound of sirens.

He was safe.

The fire fighters arrived within a minute. They

praised Tom for his quick thinking, then raced with him to the woods. The shadowed silence, and the sweet smell of the evergreens, were frightening reminders of the terrible events which had happened there, but Tom forced himself forward. He had to find Simon.

His friend lay on the trail. A ray of sunshine lit his face as Tom knelt beside him, searching for life.

Simon's eyes moved, then a low moan came from his lips. Tom was so thrilled at the sound he almost hugged him. A fire fighter approached with first-aid equipment, and Tom held his breath as she worked over Simon.

All around him were the sounds of fire fighters searching the woods for the assailant and, from the distance, the sirens of approaching emergency vehicles. Soon he was being questioned by one police officer, while a second man waited beside Simon, who was beginning to recover.

"The attacker was the same man who kidnapped Chuck," Tom said. "I remember his scruffy cowboy boots. I couldn't figure out why a security guard would wear cowboy boots."

The officer made a note, then glanced toward Simon as the boy sat up. "This kidnapper uses disguises well. You thought he was an old man?"

Tom nodded. "We were completely fooled. I really wanted to help find the puppy, because I felt sorry for it."

"There was no puppy." The officer shook his head. "A lot of kids get hurt because they fall for that trick. Someone asks them to help search for a missing animal, or a lost child, or even for pop bottles. *Never* go to a place where you can be attacked. Tell the person you have to get your parents' permission, then leave fast."

"Why did that man go after us?"

"We don't know why he's harming kids. We think he's a kidnapper, but there have been no ransom demands, so it's possible the children are dead. You and Simon could have been next."

Tom wrapped his arms around his body, feeling weak. He remained that way while Simon talked to the police, and was still feeling shaky when an officer returned from searching the woods and held out a white wig.

"Part of his disguise," she said. "We found it by a dirt road at the back of the woods. It looks as if he parked a car there, but he's long gone."

"What happens now?"

"We'll take Simon to the hospital for a check-up, and we'll drop you home."

"I'd rather go to the Big Tee."

The officer stared at Tom, then burst out laughing. "You're going to eat hamburgers, after all you've gone through?"

"Sure," Tom said. "And, anyway, I'm meeting someone important there."

"Okay, Tom, you're the boss. You kids sure are tough!"

Smiling, Tom walked beside Simon to the road. With siren wailing, a cruiser rushed them to Nelson. Tom couldn't help feeling fine as heads turned when he stepped out of the police car at the Big Tee, before it carried on to the hospital.

But his good mood was blown apart when he

entered the restaurant and Dietmar called sarcastically, "Hey, it's Mister Frank N. Stein! Come join us, Mister Stein." He was waving at Tom from a booth near the juke box. Brandi sat with him, wearing a T-shirt showing a computer picture of herself; Tom hadn't expected to share her company with Dietmar, and it took a major effort to smile when he sat down with his food.

"Hi, Brandi. How are you?"

"Okay. What's with the siren?"

Tom started to explain, but he sensed that Brandi didn't especially care, and he knew Dietmar was waiting for a chance to jeer. So he cut the story short, feeling depression cloud his spirits.

"You guys made a big mistake," Brandi said. "I wouldn't be that stupid."

"You've never blundered? Never ever?"

She shook her head, sending soft ripples through her hair. "No kidnapper could get me. I'm too smart."

Anger burned inside Tom at her arrogance. For a moment he wished the kidnapper would prove her wrong, then he realized he was being as childish as Brandi. He picked up his hot dog and ate in silence, wondering why he'd ever wanted to meet Brandi.

A group of boys made a noisy entrance into the restaurant, and Tom realized they were the Nelson players who'd lost yesterday's hockey game to Tumbler Ridge. Most seemed to know Brandi, and soon the booth was surrounded by a mob of boys, laughing and talking as they put away huge amounts of food.

The cost of their feast was shared by the team's manager, a man named George Harshbarger, and the coach, Kendall Steele, who arrived late. Nobody seemed to mind about yesterday's loss, and Simon received a lot of praise from the Nelson players.

"A friend of mine is a talent scout for Calgary," Kendall Steele told Tom. "I'll tell him to watch Simon play. He's good enough for the NHL."

"That's what I told Simon! He was talking about quitting hockey, just because of his weird coach."

Kendall Steele lit a cigarette. In the flare of the match he looked very handsome, with his light blue eyes, straight nose and carefully-trimmed moustache. "A coach like Burton Donco bothers me. He gives hockey a poor reputation, and sets a bad example for the players. An adult should be someone a youngster admires."

George Harshbarger had been talking to Brandi. Now he turned to Tom, and studied him with grim eyes. "Brandi says you and Simon were attacked this morning. I'm very glad you managed to escape. This is a terrible thing that's happening, and we all seem powerless to stop it. Why have the police refused my demand to release information about the kidnapper? They know how he operates. Why not tell the public?"

Tom studied the skin on his temples, which was unusually shiny. It looked as though George Harshbarger had recently undergone an operation, perhaps for skin cancer. Very little of his grey hair remained, and his body was thin inside his wrinkled clothing.

"The police will take care of it," Kendall Steele said, his deep voice sounding concerned. "Try not to worry, George."

"I've got kids, Kendall. They ask to play with their friends, but I'm frightened to let them out of the house. You don't have a family. You don't understand what it's like."

Brandi sipped her drink. "My brothers are away at camp. Thank goodness they're safe."

"I wrote to the police," George Harshbarger said, "and offered my help. They turned me down." He looked very upset. Tension was in the air. The juke box played on, but was ignored. The hockey players were quiet, looking at George Harshbarger.

"You could play detective," Kendall Steele said with sympathy, "and go search for a man with a fake security guard's uniform and a gold badge in his wallet, but I think you should stick to *spelunking*. Don't brood about it, George."

"What's *spelunking?*" Tom asked.

"Cave exploring. That's what George and I do for a hobby."

"Around here?"

"Ever heard of the Cody Caves? We're taking an expedition into them on Friday. Like to join us?"

"For sure! I've never been inside a cave."

Kendall Steele laughed. "It's an unforgettable experience."

He was right. Tom would never forget what happened in Cody Caves.

5

"Is a man trapped in there?"

Tattoo pointed at the dam which lay across Kootenay River. White water rushed over the spillway, and thick power lines carried electricity away from its generating station.

"They say the man was caught inside the dam during construction. On quiet nights, when the moon is bright, you can hear the *clink-clink* of his hammer as he tries to dig his way out."

The Maestro nodded his approval. "A good story,

Tattoo. You can be the guide when I open up this area to tourists. *Theolonius P. Judd presents Ghosts of the Silvery Slocan!* I can see it all now."

As the Maestro closed his eyes to dream, Tattoo turned the car at a junction and headed north into the Slocan Valley. The entire group from *Shirleen's Place* was heading for the ghost towns of the mountains, and Great Granny was wild with excitement.

"The stories I could tell!" she exclaimed, her blue eyes bright. "When the first silver was found, prospectors stampeded in from all over the world. Tinhorns, outlaws, mule skinners, remittance men, tenderfeet, the works! In Sandon there were 24 hotels and 23 saloons, and it was wild. The police only slept by day, and some mighty nasty men swung for their crimes."

Tom looked out at the swiftly-flowing river; early morning sunshine turned the trees along its banks a pale gold, and lit the crystal dew which clung to tall grass beside the highway. Rising above the narrow valley were the mountains, very high, very green and very beautiful. "Execution of criminals, in a tranquil place like this? I doubt it."

"People in Nelson used to attend public hangings in the yard of the provincial jail. Chain gangs of convicts repaired the streets. They all wore leg irons, including the women. Those were the days!"

Brandi smiled at her with affection. "It sounds pretty gross."

"But it worked! When I was young the children were safe. No one kidnapped them, or choked them in the woods."

Tom shivered, remembering the attack on Simon. Happily, his friend had been released from hospital

40

and was ready for action with his hockey team. "I heard on the news that Simon may win Most Valuable Player."

"Is he that good?" Tattoo asked.

"For sure! Come to his game tonight, Tattoo."

"Big deal," the man grunted. He looked rough this morning, with black stubble on his chin, heavy pouches under his bloodshot eyes, and hair that hadn't seen a comb for days. The back of his T-shirt said *Loose as a moose* but the words weren't true. He was, in fact, screwed up tight with tension.

"Simon may play pro hockey," Tom said. "Kendall Steele is arranging to have him scouted."

"I repeat, big deal. Let's drop the hockey talk."

"Sorry," Tom mumbled, feeling his ears glow with embarrassment. "I thought you were interested in Simon."

"Well, you were wrong."

Tom almost said *sorry* again, but stopped himself. Instead he watched the twisting highway, which plunged back and forth from sunshine to a mountain's black shadow and then back to sunshine. Straight ahead, a tree shimmered against the backdrop of the dark mountain, all its leaves on fire in the golden light of morning.

"When do we reach those ghost towns?"

"It won't be long," Great Granny answered.

"What kind of people got hanged?"

"Bobby Sproule was one. He was the prospector who discovered a massive vein of silver but lost it in a court battle to Thomas Hammill. Bobby lay in wait at the claim, shot Hammill dead, and rode like a demon for the American border. He didn't make it."

41

"Were a lot of Americans up here mining?"

"You bet. For a time the post office put U.S. stamps on letters, and July 4 was the big rip-snorting holiday. Hotels in Sandon had names like the Denver and the Virginia. When silver prices crashed, five Spokane banks went belly-up. Most miners went home, and the towns died. Sad."

"What's left in the ghost towns?"

"For me, a lot of memories. For you, old buildings to explore. Ancient coins, tobacco tins, poker chips of solid ivory, all waiting to be found. Rusting mine machinery, the wreckage of the railways, cemeteries with weathered tombstones almost impossible to read."

The Maestro smiled at her. "Sheer poetry, Euphemia. Perhaps you'll write my promotion brochures?"

"Not a chance. I can't bear the thought of tourists driving into Sandon in their campers and Winnebagos. You should leave the past alone!"

"Not when there's a dollar to be made."

Tom's eyes were stabbed by sunlight reflecting from the aluminum roof of a barn near the river. Much of the valley had been logged, and now the green water surged past farms and small clusters of houses. Tom noticed a school bus parked in one farm yard, then looked at a herd of cows on the riverbank, their white faces almost buried in the tall grass they were eating.

"The good life!" he said. "You must love it here, Tattoo."

"It's okay."

"Did you grow up in the Kootenays?"

"Nope."

Shirleen turned to smile at Tom. "When Tattoo's in a mood, look out! No sense trying to cheer him up, but I'm glad you tried. Anyway, to answer your question, he came to Nelson a year ago."

"Is that all? But he knows so much about this area."

"My guy loves history. He's always reading some kind of book."

Tattoo shook his shaggy head. "Stop talking about me. It drives me strange."

Brandi laughed. "What a temper."

"Button your lip, kid. You've been getting on my nerves lately."

"You can't talk to me like that. You're not my father."

"If I was, I'd teach you a few manners."

Shirleen started to protest, but Brandi cut her off. "Watch how you talk to me, or I'll make Mom kick you out. And don't think I can't."

"Maybe *you* should get out. I'm sick of the way you hang around."

"It's my house!"

"Yeah? Well, maybe I should get rid of you!"

Fortunately, this argument was brought to a sudden end as they rounded a bend and saw cars stopped on the highway. A police car stood by the road, lights spinning, and officers were leaning in car windows.

"Not another roadblock!" Tattoo shouted. "This is ridiculous."

Brandi leaned toward him, her eyes still on fire. "Don't you want them to catch that guy?"

"All I know is, these cops keep wrecking my day."

"Why don't you take a swing at them? Then you'll be in the slammer, and we'll all be happy."

"Drop it," Tattoo muttered angrily.

The questioning of cars ahead seemed to take a long time, and the line moved forward very slowly. In a nearby field, a group of lean young horses was grazing, their coats luxuriant in the sunshine. Suddenly one of them bolted toward the river bank and the others joined in the game, hoofs pounding the soil, manes streaming, tails raised in the joy of the moment. Then the fun ended as quickly as it had begun, and the horses returned to their grazing.

"Hey!" Tom said. "Catch that el-swanko car, and look who owns it!"

Stopped on the opposite side of the highway was a low-slung white Cadillac with chrome so bright it blinded, and a personalized license plate which read TOO COOL. Standing beside the car's open trunk, arguing with an officer, was Burton Donco.

"That guy is Simon's hockey coach. He's about as low as a snake's belly."

Tattoo had begun answering police questions, but Tom concentrated on Burton Donco. The man's meaty face looked flustered, and even a bit scared, as he talked to the officer, who was holding a wrench which she'd taken from the trunk of the big Cadillac. Finally, after a long discussion, Burton Donco took out his wallet with great reluctance and handed it to the officer.

"There's no one travelling with him," Tom said, as Tattoo put the car in gear and they spluttered away from the roadblock. "I wonder what's going on?"

No answer was obvious, and Burton Donco was soon forgotten as the highway climbed the rocky face of a mountain, then crawled along high above a blue lake. In part the scene was startling in its beauty, and in part it was very frightening, because the road narrowed to a single lane which had been blasted out of the cliff. Even Tattoo looked worried as the car crept around blind corners, below it a long drop into oblivion.

"We did it!" Tattoo said with relief, as the cliff drive ended and the road returned to normal. "That road always gives me the shivers."

Tom shook his head. "What a nightmare. I wonder how Burton Donco got his Caddy around those corners?"

"That's Slocan Lake," Great Granny said, gesturing at the azure waters far below. "Somewhere down there is a fortune in silver bars, just waiting to be found."

"Treasure?" Dietmar said, showing his first interest that day. "Could we find it?"

"That's possible, but it's under 20 fathoms of water."

"How'd it get there?"

"In 1904 a company barge was caught in a violent storm on the lake. A boxcar broke free, smashed through the guard rail, and plunged to the bottom. It was loaded with more than 100 silver ingots, worth so much that two separate expeditions have gone after them."

"They didn't succeed?"

"One group got a cable around the boxcar, and raised it. You can imagine the excitement when it split the surface, streaming mud, and all that silver was waiting inside. Then the cable broke! The boxcar went to the bottom, and was left in peace for another 30 years."

"And then?"

"A diver went down, located the boxcar, and managed to get an ingot out. Great excitement when the ingot reached the boat waiting on the surface. The diver kept pulling out bars of silver, but the boxcar was resting on a slope and he feared it would slide deeper, trapping him. So he quit, and the remaining silver is still down there. Care to search for it, Dietmar?"

"Naw. Too much work. I thought the treasure was just in the bush somewhere, lying under a tree."

Shortly after, they pulled into New Denver. At one time, Great Granny said, twelve thousand miners lived a roaring existence here, but now the only creatures moving on the sunny, leafy main street were two dogs which trotted happily past the false-fronted wooden buildings. Eventually the group found a cafe and went inside. It was low and dark, and a pop cooler hummed in one corner.

Brandi put her hand on Tom's arm as they walked to a table. "Don't you hate being a stranger?" she whispered. "Those people are all staring."

"You're right. I bet that owner's going to shout *no tourists!*"

But the man was friendly, and the food was delicious. Tom ordered a Heritage Dog, which came on a whole wheat bun with melted cheese, a strip of bacon and onions. Chewing busily, he studied the other diners.

"Those men look like prospectors, with their wooly beards. Too bad the silver rush is over."

"Some people are still making money," Shirleen said. "Four guys just found a chunk of galena contain-

46

ing five thousands dollars worth of silver. If they can locate the vein it came from, they'll be millionaires."

"I wouldn't mind visiting an old mine."

"There's lots of them in the mountains, but they're dangerous. Rocks and beams could fall on your head."

Dietmar rapped Tom's head with his knuckles. "No problem for Austen. That skull's solid marble."

Laughing, the Maestro called for coffee. Quickly Tom reached into his pocket for a special sugar cube he'd bought in a Nelson joke shop. When the coffee arrived, he distracted the Maestro's attention long enough to drop the cube into his cup.

"What's left at Sandon?" he asked Great Granny. "Is there a lot to see?"

She shook her head. "A flood smashed the town in 1955 and turned it into a pile of old lumber. But there's a few buildings still standing. One of them . . . "

"Faugh!" the Maestro cried, staring at his coffee. Floating on the surface was a maggot, glistening and horrible. As everyone gazed in shock, Tom lifted out the maggot with a spoon and dropped it on Dietmar's plate.

"It's only plastic. Naughty boy, Oban."

"What are you talking about?"

"Shouldn't put trick sugar cubes in your uncle's coffee."

"I didn't . . . "

The Maestro cut him off. "I'll speak to you later, young man," he said, frowning. "My heart's too weak for such a shock."

As everyone got up from the table, Dietmar shoved his fist into Tom's face. "Revenge will be mine,

Austen, and it will be sweet."

"I'm shaking in my booties."

From New Denver they drove high into the mountains, then followed a dirt road toward Sandon. Great Granny pointed out a former railway route, carved out of high cliffs, just before they drove into the ghost town.

"It's not what I expected," Tom said, looking at the few old buildings by a creek. "I thought there'd be a fancy opera house, and boardwalks with strolling old-timers, and maybe a jail with bullet holes in the walls."

The Maestro took out a notepad, and wrote busily. "All good ideas, Tom. When I take over Sandon, I'll have the finest designers create it all. Maybe we'll even stage a shoot-out, every day at high noon."

"What rubbish," Great Granny said. "Use your imagination, Tom. That empty building facing the creek was once the Virginia, Sandon's finest hotel. In the lobby were aspidistras, big and green, and brass spittoons that were polished every day. Upstairs, people slept in feather beds and used porcelain chamber pots imported from Britain."

"What's a chamber pot?"

"There were no indoor bathrooms. In the night you used a chamber pot, which was kept hidden under the bed."

Brandi giggled. "How disgusting. What were the outhouses like in winter?"

"Pure agony. Snow drifted into them, and there was frost on the seat."

"Yikes!"

"A friend of mine, Axe Handle Nell, was sitting in an

48

outhouse when it was pushed over by a gang of boys. She lit out after them with her shotgun, but it was all in fun. The things we laughed about over our skee."

"What's that?"

"Whisky."

"What did you eat?"

"Moose burgers were my favourite, with a big hunk of sourdough bread and a mug of sarsaparilla to wash it down. Mulligan stew tasted good after a lot of dancing, and then we'd head for the wet grocery department."

"Which was?"

"The bar. If you could have seen it! Solid mahogany, with plate-glass mirrors and a handlebar-moustached bartender always willing to listen to a sad story."

"But you said it was all fun, Great Granny."

"Some terrible tragedies occurred here, Brandi." She pointed at the surrounding mountains. "All the mines were high up there, at the end of narrow trails. In winter the snow was something fierce, but the boys still broke a trail to Sandon to have some fun. One Christmas Eve, five of them were buried alive by an avalanche, and they weren't the only victims. Explosions in the mines wiped out some good people."

"How'd they get the ore down from the mines?"

"It was towed out on rawhide by horses. When the snow got deep, they put snowshoes on the horses and kept right on working. The Payne Boy Mine turned a profit of four million dollars, but many miners were permanently broke."

"Didn't they get paid?"

"Sure, but they'd come down to Sandon with their pay packets, join a game of poker and lose it all. Some sharp operators played at the tables, always with their backs to the wall for protection. On Sunday morning at church they'd put poker chips in the collection plate."

"That wasn't very nice."

"Oh, the minister just smiled and cashed the chips!" Great Granny pointed at the car. "Tattoo is looking impatient, so we'd better push off. I feel so much younger, talking about my past. Thanks, kids."

Brandi put her arms around Great Granny, and hugged her frail body. "I love you," she said gently. "You're the best thing in my life."

Tom left them alone, and went to kneel by the creek. The mountain water numbed his hands as he cupped them to drink. The taste was pure and fresh, so icy his teeth ached. The water ran swiftly over the many white stones on the creek bed, sounding different notes and rhythms where it rushed over a fallen log in a miniature waterfall, or curled around a boulder's edge to form a pool that was deep and clear. As a dead leaf twirled down to ripple the surface of the pool, the car's horn blasted.

"Let's go!" Tattoo shouted. "We're getting hot, sitting here waiting."

Soon they were back on the main highway, rushing through a canyon with steep walls that shut out the afternoon sun. Somehow the tires managed to avoid the black butterflies which kept coming out of nowhere.

"There's still no ransom demand," Shirleen said, biting one of her fingernails. "The families of those kids are going through agony. I heard that a psychic is flying in from Los Angeles to help in the search. Surely all this will end soon."

"Let's hope the ending is happy," Brandi said. "I'm so glad the boys are safe at summer camp."

Shirleen turned to her. "There's still you to worry about."

"Oh Mom, won't you quit? I can take care of myself."

Tattoo was staring at Brandi in the mirror. The man didn't say anything, just studied her beautiful face, then shook his head. A few minutes later he stopped the car in an open valley, where a collection of old mine buildings had been flooded by beaver ponds. The grey wood and rusty roofs looked so forlorn that Tom sighed.

"It's kind of sad, thinking about all the people who lived here. They've just disappeared, like dust, after coming to the Slocan with such hopes. I wonder what happened to them after the mines failed? Maybe they lost everything, and ended up living on Skid Road."

"They tried their best," the Maestro said, "and enjoyed each day. That's what counts."

Everyone got out to stretch except Tattoo, who remained slumped behind the wheel, his eyes on Brandi. Tom gazed at the beaver lodges, then skipped some stones over the blue water before going to watch Shirleen take a picture of Brandi and Great Granny, with the wrecked mine buildings as background.

"You mentioned there were railways here," he said to Great Granny, "but I just can't imagine a freight whistling through this empty valley."

"They built the *Kaslo & Slocan* right past here, racing the CPR to lay the first rail into Sandon and claim all that ore-hauling business. The CPR won, but the K&S got its revenge. In the middle of the night

51

they wrapped a cable around the CPR station in Sandon, hooked it to a wood-burning locomotive, and pulled the station into the creek. Those CPR boys were hopping mad!"

Tom kept watch for signs of the railway as they continued to travel east, and finally spotted the splintered timbers of a trestle just as they entered the next ghost town. There was much more to see here, including the foundation and roof of a house missing all its walls.

"Maybe termites ate the walls," he said. "Look at that old hotel, with the stairs leading up to nowhere. Do you think a wind blew off the top floor?"

"Old Chester may have used it for firewood," Tattoo answered, screeching to a stop in clouds of dust.

"Who's Old Chester?"

"He stayed here in Retallack long after the mine shut down in '52. Other folks moved out, and cougars came nosing around, but Old Chester refused to believe the town had died. Some say his spirit still prowls these buildings."

"Let's explore this place. It sounds great."

Stepping into the baking hot sun, Tom studied the ruins of a pickup truck. Its windshield was laced with fine cracks like a spider's web, the hood was up to reveal a missing engine, and the headlight sockets hung uselessly. The axles were broken, and little remained of the tires.

Near the truck was a house with empty black windows, weathered walls and long streaks of rust staining the tin roof. As a swallow flew out of an upstairs window, Tom grabbed Tattoo's arm.

"Look! Someone's hiding up there."

Every head snapped toward the old house, and they all strained to see into the darkness. Another swallow flew into the sunshine, and then Tattoo smiled.

"It's just an old curtain, billowing beside the window. Good trick, Tom. You had me fooled."

Tom forced a smile, and managed to pretend he hadn't been scared. Then he saw Dietmar's face; there was no fooling him. "Let's come back one night, and track down Old Chester's ghost. What do you say, Dietmar?"

"Forget it."

The Maestro took out his notepad. "Notice that old log cabin. Normally I'd restore the roof and set up a Gourmet Flapjack Dining Lounge, but I've got a different idea. Do you· see how pretty the cabin is, framed between the trees with the river bubbling past?"

Shirleen nodded. "I think I'll take its picture."

"You confirm my plan, dear lady! What I propose is a series of Photo Opportunity Spots throughout the Silvery Slocan. There'll be a sign saying *Take a memorable picture from here*, with an arrow showing which way to point your camera."

"How do you make money from that?"

"I fence off the spot and charge admission. Pay your dollar, then take your picture."

She laughed. "Then I'd better get mine now, before that fence goes up." She went to the car, then turned with an upset face. "I forgot my camera at Zincton! I must have left it on a stump."

Tattoo swore angrily. "Now we have to drive all the way back. Thanks a lot, Shirleen."

"I'll pay the gas."

"Don't bother, but next time use your brains."

As everyone returned to the car, Tom gazed unhappily at the deserted buildings he'd wanted to explore. "May I stay here, and poke around?"

"Suit yourself," Tattoo said, gunning the engine.

Dietmar looked at Tom for a moment, then said, "I'll stay, too."

"Why? Retallack doesn't interest you."

"How do you know, Austen? We might meet Old Chester's ghost."

Tom shrugged. He waved as the car drove away, then went to examine some machinery which had turned to solid rust. Beside it were piles of twisted rails. "I wonder if this used to be an underground railway, for hauling ore out of the mine?"

Dietmar grunted, already bored. Tom shook his head, wishing he was alone, then walked to a shed where racks of trays were filled with rock borings. The rotten floor was filled with holes, and a wind blew through cracks in the walls. Outside the window, the leaves of a poplar made a sad sound as they rustled.

"This is a lonely place. I hope Tattoo won't be long."

"He may not return," Dietmar said. "Have you thought of that?"

"What do you mean?"

"Maybe Tattoo and Shirleen faked that act about the camera. They could be planning to bump off the Maestro, then head for the American border with his money."

Tom tried to laugh. "What a stupid story."

"Can we trust Tattoo? We hardly know the guy, and now he's left us alone in the wilderness. If he doesn't return, how will we get home? It'll soon be dark, and then the bears come down the mountains. Not to mention Old Chester."

"I don't believe in ghosts," Tom protested, even though secretly he did. Suddenly he felt cold, and went outside into the sunshine. The mountains no longer looked so friendly, and he couldn't help staring at the black window where he'd seen the moving shape. Had it really been a billowing curtain? That's what Tattoo had said, but maybe he was lying. Someone might be lurking in the old house, watching them from the darkness.

Watching and waiting.

Tom turned his back on the house and walked away, whistling bravely. Nothing was going to spoil his day. He headed for a nearby building that looked worth exploring; its walls had turned black with age, and there was a hole in the roof where a chimney had once poked out.

Through a crooked space which used to be a door, Tom saw the remains of a stove leaning against the wall. Linoleum peeled up from the floor and a pair of filthy jeans hung from a nail. As Tom worked up the courage to go inside, swallows left their nests on the walls and shot past his head, making anguished cries.

Something moved above the door, then a furry shape emerged from a narrow cavity. A bat! It fluttered around Tom's head before returning to the wall, where it hung upside down with legs spread, looking like a large spider. Its head moved slowly back and forth as it watched Tom.

"Isn't that something, Oban?"

Tom backed away, keeping his eyes on the bat as he

waited for Dietmar to say something. But there was no reply. Tom turned and found emptiness. Dietmar had vanished.

Suspecting a trick, Tom walked slowly back to the shed, expecting Dietmar to leap out of hiding or bounce a rock off a wall near his head. Somewhere a door slammed, making Tom jump. Was it the wind?

"Okay, Oban, you've got me nervous. Congratulations."

Branches rattled above Tom's head. He remembered the death's head in the woods, then the man choking Simon. It had been so frightening.

"Give it up, Oban. So you've got me scared, big deal! You want a hero's medal? You'd better come out of hiding, because we shouldn't get separated in a place like this. Don't forget that a creepy kidnapper is on the loose."

Tom's words echoed from a nearby hillside, bouncing back in shrill tones that mocked his fear. They were followed by silence, complete and ominous. Nothing moved, and there was no sign of the car returning. If Dietmar had been captured, he might be dead before help came.

Tom knew he must locate Dietmar immediately. Either he had to get him free, or be able to tell the others where Dietmar was being held. He knew there was no time to lose, but it still took enormous courage to enter the nearest building.

Probably it had been a miners' bunkhouse, for it was very large. The musty smell wrinkled Tom's nose, and broken glass snapped underfoot as he tip-toed into a room where a screen hung in shreds over a window. On a wooden table was an ancient typewriter, its keys crushed as though someone had battered them with an enormous sledgehammer.

Suddenly Tom whirled around, certain that fingers were reaching for his throat, but nothing moved. Cold air crept inside his clothes, making him shiver as he walked down the hallway to another room. Here an enormous hole gaped in the wall, as if a bomb had blown it apart. Wood hung down from the hole, and wind blew through it to scatter the paper which littered the floor.

SLAM!

The noise came from upstairs, so loud that Tom's heart leapt. His eyes scanned the ceiling, waiting for footsteps, but none came. Only groans and creaks sounded from the old building as it waited for Tom to discover its secret.

With a rapidly beating heart, he approached the staircase. Pausing, Tom waited for noises from above, then forced himself on. If he didn't keep moving, he knew terror would freeze him to the spot.

The staircase twisted up into shadows, making it almost impossible to see. Tom climbed slowly, step by step, forcing his eyes to search the dark air. He found a long hallway where two rows of doors waited, some open, some closed. A mattress lay in one, most of its stuffing torn away by mice making nests. In another room, bed springs leaned against the wall; rust had run down from them, marking the wall with an evil stain that looked like blood.

Was Dietmar already dead?

Horror overwhelmed Tom. He turned and ran, fear pounding through his body, his mouth gasping, all his being intent on reaching safety. Racing down the hallway, he reached the staircase and plunged down, ignoring the noise he made as he stumbled through the darkness toward the outside door. Flinging it open, Tom dashed outside.

He was free, but he couldn't tear his eyes away from the building. As he ran on, Tom searched the blank windows for pursuing demons.

Then, at that very moment, he was seized by two powerful hands.

6

Tom shouted in alarm.

With all his strength, he fought to escape the hands which gripped him. Then he looked up at the man's face, and stared in shock.

It was Tattoo.

His teeth were clenched, and sweat shone in glistening droplets on his skin. "Relax!" he yelled. "Just take it easy."

"Leave me alone!"

"Not until you calm down. What happened in that

building? Your face is so pale, I'd swear you've seen a ghost."

Tom continued to fight Tattoo, then realized he had to trust the man. "Someone's got Dietmar. We've got to find him, right away."

"Dietmar?" Tattoo released Tom, and his lips spread slowly in a smile. "Why? What happened?"

Puzzled by the smile, Tom quickly explained. By the time he was finished, Tattoo was laughing so hard that Tom's face was red with embarrassment. What was going on?

Finally the man calmed down. "Remember the cafe in New Denver? I saw you put that trick sugar in the Maestro's coffee."

"So what?"

"I think Dietmar just got his revenge."

Turning toward the old building, Tom saw Dietmar leaning in the doorway with a big grin on his face. "Planning to enter the Olympics, Austen? You're fast enough to win some golds for Canada."

"You slammed those doors?"

"Good work, Sherlock. You figured it out."

Anger boiled inside Tom, remembering what he'd gone through trying to help Dietmar. He clenched his fists, ready to have it out, then abruptly turned his back and walked to the waiting car.

All the way home he suffered through the joking remarks and the chuckles, thankful only that Brandi refused to join in the fun. In fact, she blasted Dietmar for being "ignorant", making Tom feel good for about 60 seconds. Then he lapsed into misery, knowing the story would be a hit at Queenston School when they returned to Winnipeg.

Fortunately, Dietmar refused to join the trip to Cody Caves next day, and was left behind when a convoy of 4x4 vehicles headed north in brilliant sunshine. Across Kootenay Lake was a perfect view of the blue Purcell Mountains, standing side by side all the way into the far distance; the forest was thick, broken only once by a tiny town which somehow clung to life in the wilderness.

"This is Ainsworth," Kendall Steele said. "Later today we'll stop here for a swim in the hot springs pool."

"Sounds great."

"That's the Silver Ledge Hotel," he said, pointing along a side street at a perfectly preserved frontier hotel with wooden balconies along each of its floors. "It's a museum now, but for 15 years it stood empty and not even a window was broken, even though it was full of valuable antique furniture. An upright piano, a swivel chair and desk, leather armchairs; you name it, they all survived."

George Harshbarger grunted. "That wouldn't happen today. Kids would break in, and clean out everything."

"Why kids?" Tattoo asked.

"Vandalism everywhere." George Harshbarger stared moodily across the lake as they left Ainsworth behind. "My store's had three break-ins."

"You wanna relax about it, George." The 4x4 whined as Kendall Steele shifted gears. "Don't you have insurance?"

"Makes no difference."

Kendall Steele smiled and lit another cigarette, adding to the pollution inside the 4x4. "My boy will never be a vandal. I'll see to that."

George Harshbarger looked surprised. "What . . ."

"Hey," Tattoo said, "would someone open a window? I don't smoke, and I'm dying back here."

Kendall Steele obeyed the request, and fresh mountain air swept into the 4x4. Turning off the highway, they started climbing the steep gravel road which led to Cody Caves. Trees grew close around, and moss hung down from branches, looking like scraggly green hair. Tom leaned forward, wondering what lay ahead.

"I can't wait to see the caves. It'll be just like *Tom Sawyer*, all those big echoing caverns and smoky candles. Let's hope we don't get lost."

George Harshbarger shook his head. "You've got the wrong idea about these caves, son. I just hope your nerves are strong. Most kids today couldn't handle the pressures of Cody."

"Why? Are the caves dangerous?"

"Get lost in there, and in two hours you'll be dead of hypothermia."

"What's that?"

"Loss of body temperature. It's cold in the caves, with 100 percent humidity. Your hands and feet go numb, followed by uncontrollable shivering, then you lose the ability to think clearly. A terrible death, in exactly two hours."

Kendall Steele laughed. "You're in a glum mood today, George. Nobody has ever died in Cody Caves."

"There's always a first time."

"Don't worry, Tom, you'll love this experience. You're heading outta reality, beyond the twilight zone into perpetual darkness. Like those who become blind, your other senses will leap into sharp focus. Smell, touch, hearing are all so intense."

"We won't be able to see?"

"Sure, there'll be a miner's lamp on the hard hat you'll be wearing. But be sure to switch it off once, just to experience a total visual eclipse."

The 4x4 roared as Kendall Steele shifted gears. The big wheels powered through a mud hole, splattering the windshield with wet brown globs. The dark tunnel of trees ended abruptly and far below they saw the lake, looking like a blue puddle. For a few seconds they glimpsed the jagged mountains, looking spectacular with their glaciers white in the sun, and then the view was lost as the road veered suddenly around a cliff and climbed straight up into the forest. Tom hung on tightly as the 4x4 leapt a gravel trench and landed with a thud that scattered the mess of clothing on the floor. A hard hat, mud-caked overalls, cast-off jeans and a pair of grimy cowboy boots, even a squashed cowboy hat, all slid across the floor as the 4x4 fought its way up the mountainside.

"We're in the middle of nowhere," Tom said. "How'd these caves ever get discovered?"

"Fellow named Henry Cody came out from Prince Edward Island in 1886. A huge man, but gentle. Once a miner took a shot at him and the bullet went through both of Cody's cheeks. Instead of killing the man with his bare hands, Cody spun him in the air a couple of times, then threw him to the floor. What self-control! Another time Cody was down a mine shaft with a fellow worker. They lit the fuses for a series of blasts, then discovered someone had foolishly pulled up their escape ladder. Cody grabbed his companion, tossed him up the shaft to safety, then saved himself by sheltering behind broken rock. The world will never see a man like that again."

"Henry Cody found these caves?"

"Yup. Probably while prospecting."

"That was the beginning of the end for the caves," Kendall Steele said sadly. "In only one century, man has destroyed what nature took millions of years to create. Muddy boots have tracked across white crystal-line flowstone floors, crunching down miniature dams. People have broken off stalactites and soda straws as souvenirs, or painted their names on the walls. Total ignorance."

"What's a soda straw?"

"It's a hollow stalactite, **grow**ing from the ceiling crystal by crystal. Dripwater carries dissolved lime-stone down, and calcite is deposited at a rate of a cubic centimetre a century. It's slow progress, but so beautiful."

"Correct, my friend," George Harshbarger said, pat-ting his shoulder, "and let's not forget that most of the caves haven't been harmed by visitors."

"You're right. There's hope yet."

Stopping in the forest clearing, the 4x4 was joined by the other vehicles bringing the rest of the expedi-tion. Kendall Steele and George Harshbarger super-vised the preparations, giving each person a pair of coveralls and a hard hat with a lamp; a wire connected the lamp to a battery in the pocket of the coveralls.

The men seemed prepared for any emergency. In addition to matches in a watertight container, they had whistles, emergency food parcels, waterproof heavy-duty lights and a sealed thermometer. "You must expect the worst," Tom said nervously, wondering what lay ahead.

"I want you to relax, Tom, and overcome your fears." Kendall Steele squeezed his shoulders with strong hands, his handsome blue eyes looking straight into Tom's. "There's a big challenge underground, using your hidden strengths to conquer the unknown. When I enter the Cody Caves with my son, I know he'll become a man. You'll have the same experience today."

"I'll give it a try, Mister Steele."

"Good boy."

Kendall Steele studied Tom's face, then turned as Tattoo approached, looking bulkier than usual in his blue coveralls. "All set?"

"I guess so." Tattoo lifted his hard hat and ran a hand over his damp forehead. "My company logged somewhere on this mountain. Aren't there several deserted mine buildings near here?"

"No." Kendall Steele waved a hand at the others. "Let's get moving."

With some reluctance, the adventurers started climbing a steep trail. The forest smells were rich and sweet, the evergreens reminding Tom of Christmas, and a small stream tumbled down nearby. Accompanied by the peeping of small birds hidden in the branches, they followed the path as it changed from wet and spongy needles to rocks and then exposed roots, their gnarled surfaces slippery underfoot.

"Here we are," George Harshbarger said at last, pointing at a narrow cleft almost hidden among the trees on a hillside.

One of the teen-agers in the expedition stared in

surprise. "I expected a proper cave. How are we supposed to fit into that little space?"

"Use your agility. Your body is going to get a real workout today."

"How about if I wait out here?"

George Harshbarger shook his head. "Don't talk rubbish."

"Okay, gang," Kendall Steele said, "listen closely. Stick together in the caves, follow our instructions, and avoid damaging the formations. If your light goes out, and you're alone, you'll be in danger of getting lost. Stay in one place and wait for help. Now switch on those lights, and follow me."

He bent sideways, then wiggled through the cleft and disappeared from sight. After Tattoo squeezed through, Tom followed. "Is it ever dark," he whispered, as he tried to get his footing on the big rocks which sloped down into a cavern. The yellow beam of light from his hard hat darted around the walls, then stopped at a wriggling brown lump.

"Wow! That looks like a million spiders, all bunched together."

"They're Harvestman spiders, hibernating. Your light is disturbing them, so move it away."

The air was damp and cold, and seemed to smell of muddy water. Tom's breath rose in a mist through the yellow beam as he followed the other lights to the far side of the cavern. Kneeling down, he squeezed into an opening in the rocks, and was immediately overcome by claustrophobia as he found himself in a narrow tunnel through which he had to crawl. Half way along, he stopped moving, fighting to catch his breath, then forced himself forward.

Tom's hard hat smashed against the tunnel roof with a *clang!* that made his ears ring, then he finally reached the end and was able to stand up. Already he was covered in mud, and he wondered if he'd ever see daylight again.

"How are you doing, Tattoo?"

"Okay," the man grunted, getting slowly to his feet. "I thought I was going to get stuck in there. When do we go home?"

Tom smiled. "Kendall Steele said you'll discover your hidden strengths today."

"The only strength I need is to pop open a beer. I wish there was one in my hand right now."

The expedition had reached a large passage which echoed with the sound of a stream rushing through. As the teen-agers moved along a narrow path above the water, one of them stepped too close to the edge and his arms swung wildly as he fought to keep his balance.

"Say gang," Kendall Steele called, "did I tell you these are poison rocks?"

"How come?"

"One drop will kill you."

There was scattered laughter, then a voice called, "What caused these caves?"

"You're surrounded by limestone. Long ago, tens of thousands of years, water crept into cracks in this limestone and began eating it away. Eventually there was a stream moving along the fissures, which became wider and wider as walls and ceilings collapsed."

"If you listen carefully," George Harshbarger said, "you'll hear how the caves are still being changed.

Each drop of water that falls from the ceiling will precipitate a few crystals of calcite, slowly creating those stalactites and stalagmites."

He swung his light to show the icicle-like formations which glistened with condensation, then pointed at the hollow soda straws clustered on the ceiling. "Imagine what has happened in the world outside while those soda straws have been growing. Wars, floods, famines, the birth and death of great civilizations. Meanwhile, these very soda straws have slowly taken shape on the ceiling. Isn't that amazing?"

"I can see you guys love this place," Tattoo said, "but I'm freaked."

"Why?"

"Because the air in here tastes of dirt. Because I feel like I'm a prisoner in a dungeon. Because maybe I'll never smell a fresh breeze again, or see the sunshine on trees. It's dumb, but I feel scared."

"You'll get out safely."

"What if there's an earthquake, and the entrance gets sealed by a rock fall? We'll suffocate, just like miners who get trapped underground."

"You're safe with us," George Harshbarger said impatiently. "I give you my personal guarantee."

Turning, he led the way to a shaft which rose above their heads. Scrambling from handhold to handhold, the group worked its way up the shaft, while the sound of the stream faded away behind them. One of the climbers knocked a rock loose, and it crashed down past Tom's head. As water ran down his neck, he realized his greatest desire was to get out of the caves, never to return.

Reaching a passage just large enough to sit up in,

the expedition stopped to rest. Above Tom's head were shapes that looked like petrified white slugs, glistening in the shaft of light from his hard hat. Moving the light slowly, he discovered other forms resembling thin white spiders, and snails with tiny horns, all shaped from calcite over the centuries.

"This place is kind of neat, when you stop to look."

"You're right," Kendall Steele said, "and you haven't yet seen a cave pearl, or a fried egg. Those formations are so beautiful, they'll knock your eyes out."

"Any bats in here?"

"Only in winter, when they're hibernating." He bent his head, listening. "Do you hear the dripping water? It's been falling like that for one million years."

Tom's fingertips were cold and he felt hungry. Although he wanted to keep resting there was no stopping George Harshbarger, who led the group deeper into the caves. Again claustrophobia overwhelmed Tom as he slithered down a muddy passage. With the rocky walls pressing close around, he had to lie on his side and heave himself along a low tunnel while water dripped on his face and his heart beat rapidly.

"You know what?" he said to Tattoo, as the man wriggled free of the tunnel. "Before we get out of the caves, we have to follow these passages all the way back. How deep is George Harshbarger taking us?"

"Right to China. If I ever see sunshine again, I'll kiss the sky."

"Those brown formations look like huge veins. Maybe we're inside some giant's lungs."

"Let's hope the giant doesn't light up a cigarette."

They reached a larger cave, where the darting lights from the hard hats made shadows which leapt and faded on the rocky walls. Strange shapes and colours were everywhere. A calcite formation resembled a butterfly clinging to the pale limestone wall, a long white snake seemed to twist across the ceiling, and other translucent figures created scenes of crystal beauty.

"Who feels like a special adventure?" George Harshbarger asked. Tattoo groaned, but the teen-agers shouted their agreement. "What I've got in mind is a chimney squeeze. One at a time, you crawl up a tiny side passage, as high as possible, then wait for the others. The record is 12 people stuffed inside a chimney."

"If we get stuck, we'll die in there!"

"Sure, and a century from now they'll bring out your skeletons, bone by bone, and reassemble them at the Ainsworth museum."

"What a jigsaw puzzle!"

The group headed off with happy faces, but Tattoo remained behind, slumped on a rock. "Enjoy yourself, Tom. I'm staying here."

"Want some company?"

"Sure. I wouldn't mind."

Sitting down, Tom listened to the voices of the teen-agers become muffled, then die away in the distance. Silence came to the cave, broken only by the drip of water on rock. Cold and loneliness spread through Tom's tired body.

Suddenly Tattoo's hand lashed out. Seizing the cord from Tom's light, he ripped it loose. At the same moment, he switched off his own lamp, and they were plunged into absolute darkness.

"Hey! What's going on?"

There was no reply. The silence was terrible as Tom fumbled with his light, trying to find the cord, his hands shaking uncontrollably. Turning toward Tattoo he tried desperately to see the man, but found only black air and a weird pattern of bright designs that seemed to pop and fizz in front of his useless eyes.

Sensing somehow that he mustn't speak, Tom started to edge away from Tattoo, but his foot caught on a rock and he tumbled backwards. His hard hat slammed against the cave wall with a sound that crashed inside his head, then the terrible silence returned.

Tom could no longer tell what direction was up or down. His skin crawled, his chest ached with the agony of his fear, and his eyes searched the overwhelming darkness, trying to find a way to protect himself. And then light flashed into his eyes as Tattoo switched on his lamp. Chuckling, he helped Tom up.

"Scared you, huh?"

"Why did you do that?"

"I dunno. Bored, I guess."

His body still trembling, Tom looked into Tattoo's eyes, trying to understand.

7

Kendall Steele was furious.

When he heard from Tattoo about Tom's light, he tore a strip off the man. Tattoo protested feebly that Kendall Steele had recommended trying absolute darkness, but it didn't help. By the time the expedition staggered out of the caves, Tattoo was in a foul temper.

"Look at me!" He stared in disbelief at the mud which caked his body. "I'm a mess. Why'd I ever agree to this craziness?"

Tom shrugged. His mouth was filled with the most delicious food he'd ever tasted, a simple submarine sandwich that tasted like a victory banquet. It felt so great to be in daylight, smelling the pines and gazing at the blue sky.

Tattoo yanked off his coveralls, and slammed them down. "I could have been at the Civic, drinking with my buddies. But I'll be there tonight!"

Tom looked at him in surprise. "What about the party? Is it cancelled?"

"The party was Shirleen's idea. She can have it without my help. Nobody wants me there, anyway. I'm just a fat slob with no job and no family." He gave the wheel of a 4x4 a vicious kick, then looked grimly at the surrounding forest. "I'm gonna find those old mine buildings, and live there like a hermit. I remember thinking somebody was fixing one up to live in, but I'll clear them out fast. Any argument and I'll use the boots."

Tattoo's anger and unhappiness were so intense that Tom backed away, wondering if he might become violent. But Kendall Steele hustled Tattoo into a 4x4, and very soon they were racing down the mountain.

"Are Cody Caves the world's biggest?" Tom asked.

George Harshbarger snorted. "You kids and your records. The longest fingernails, the fattest cat, the biggest cave. When I was a boy, we were too busy studying our school work to care about those things."

"The deepest are in France," Kendall Steele said. "The longest are the Mammoth Caves in Kentucky, huge bore holes that once carried rivers."

"Could you drown in a cave?"

"It's possible. Some spelunkers I know were

73

trapped when flash floods suddenly raised the level of an underground stream, sealing off the escape route. But they were rescued."

"Well, I doubt if I'll ever go back inside a cave."

"You never know, Tom."

Very soon they were at Ainsworth, their tired bodies relaxing in the hot springs pool. Next to it were caverns to explore; fascinating, but too much like the experience at Cody Caves, so Tom spent most of his time floating in the pool, trying to solve the puzzle of the missing children. Surely the truth was close at hand, but he couldn't seem to fit the pieces together.

"Do you think Tippi and Chuck are still alive?" he asked later, as the 4x4 approached Nelson's big orange highway bridge.

"No," Tattoo said glumly. "They've had it. Kaput. Finished. Gone forever."

George Harshbarger turned to look at him. "You're a very gloomy man, always seeing the bad side. Why's that?"

"It's none of your business, but life's treated me rough. I lost my job, and I don't have a family anymore."

Looking surprised, Kendall Steele stared at Tattoo in the rear view mirror.

"That's too bad," George Harshbarger said, "but other people lose their families without becoming so cynical."

Tom leaned forward. "I read in a detective magazine that some people who lose their babies steal another as a replacement. It made me feel sad."

George Harshbarger looked at Tom. "You seem a nice lad. Why aren't you playing for our hockey team?"

74

"I don't live in Nelson. I'm visiting from Winnipeg."

The man grunted. "Never seen the prairies myself. Flat, they tell me."

"We don't have the mountains, but we've got the world's friendliest people."

"More records! Attend to your school books, son, that's my advice."

"Yes sir. Who do you think will win the hockey final tonight?"

"Tumbler Ridge. No question of that."

But George Harshbarger was wrong. Despite the screaming support of the Nelson fans, the British Columbia champions went down to defeat against a powerful team from Seaside, Oregon. The only consolation came when the Most Valuable Player was announced, and Simon skated out to accept the trophy. As the crowd stood to cheer, Simon raised the glittering trophy above his head and a broad grin lit up his face.

"He's such a doll," Brandi said, as she pounded her hands together, "and he'll make a fortune in pro hockey. I wish he liked me more."

Tom smiled shyly. "How about a future with a detective?"

"No money in it. Sherlock Holmes couldn't even afford a stereo. He just played that old violin all day long."

"I guess you're right," Tom said glumly, then brightened as Simon skated over to show them the trophy. "Coming to the party, Simon?"

"You bet! Meet you there."

Shirleen's Place was a beacon in the night, with lights shining brightly and rock music throbbing from every window. Car doors slammed and people shouted greetings to friends as a stream of guests hurried up the steps and crossed the big porch to join the good times.

On each floor a different music system played at full volume, and people who weren't dancing had to shout into each other's faces to be heard. Leaning against a thundering speaker in the living room was Shirleen, dressed entirely in black with a silver cross at her throat, smiling happily as she absorbed the rhythms.

"Where's Tattoo?" Brandi screamed above the noise.

"At the Civic." Shirleen lit a cigarette. "Join the fun, kids."

Eventually Simon arrived, and received a lot of handshakes from people who had attended the hockey tournament. Tom watched jealously as Simon signed autographs, but the feeling died quickly when Simon smiled at him. He was one of the nicest people Tom had ever met.

"Congratulations again on getting MVP. How'd your coach take the loss?"

Simon sighed. "He flipped. He went absolutely bananas. I guess he figured this was the Stanley Cup or something."

Brandi made a face. "That bad, huh?"

"He's so totally insane with anger that it scares me. There's no telling what he might do."

She laughed. "Oh, I bet he's just a cream puff inside."

"I don't know, Brandi. I'm steering clear until he calms down."

Dietmar wandered into the room, feeding his face with a sandwich which featured multiple layers of salami and pickles. "Hey, you know why Tom Austen carries a turkey under his arm?"

"I don't actually care," Brandi said, "but tell me, Dietmar."

"For spare parts."

"Gross." Brandi took Simon's arm and led him out of the room, leaving Tom feeling bleak. "I'm not having much fun," he said to Dietmar. "How about you?"

"Forget Brandi, and get some food. Then you'll feel better."

"Maybe I will. Good thinking, Dietmar. Thanks."

"Okay."

The party was getting louder. The timbers of the old house shook as dancers stomped their feet, and Tom thought he heard the wailing sirens of police coming to break up the party, but the emergency was elsewhere. Eating bacon-flavoured chips from a bowl he wandered from room to room, then found Simon and Brandi at the front door.

"So long, Tom," Simon said.

"You're leaving already?"

"Yup, but I'll see you again before the team heads home next week."

The front door crashed open, and four young men of about 20 came in.

"Hiya, good people, is this Tattoo's party?" Without waiting for an answer they headed toward the music, and Simon grinned.

"It's going to be a long night."

"You bet," Brandi said. "I've never seen those guys before. I'd better make sure they don't wreck the joint."

She hurried off. After saying goodbye to Simon, Tom spent a long time on the porch. The night air was warm on his face and the music was pleasant, but eventually he felt bored and went in search of Brandi.

He found her dancing in the basement recreation room with one of the party-crashers, a man with black hair and a deep tan that suggested many hours on the beach. He had a smile which featured a lot of white teeth but no warmth, and there was something flashy and self-centred about the way he danced. Deciding he didn't look trustworthy, Tom slumped down on a sofa to watch him. Eventually the dancing ended and the man wandered away, perhaps in search of something to steal, but before Tom could follow he was joined on the sofa by Brandi.

"Having fun?"

"Sure, Brandi. This is a great party, but can your mom afford it? There's mountains of food in the kitchen."

"She's a very generous person. Right now there's money in her purse, because you guys are renting rooms, so Mom's spending it on a party for her friends. Plus Tattoo's buddies, who weren't even invited."

"How come you were dancing with that guy, if you don't know him?"

"Because he's good-looking, and a great dancer."

"Oh." Tom stared at the wall, trying to think of something to say. "Got any plans for when you finish school?"

"I'm going to study law."

"Really? My mother's a lawyer."

"Hey, maybe I could visit you some time, and meet her."

"That would be fantastic, Brandi. I'll show you around Winnipeg. You'll love it."

"That's a date," Brandi said, smiling. "You know why I'm going into law? Because so many people are victims, and I want to help them."

"You mean victims of kidnappers?"

"Not just that. I'm talking about victims of landlords who gouge on rents, or victims of bosses who fire them without any reason, or victims of governments that take away their human rights."

"I've never thought about it much."

"I have, and I'm going to fight for those people." Brandi tossed her soft hair, then stared into the distance, her face looking troubled.

"Cheer up! This is a party."

"You're right." She jumped up, and smiled at Tom. "Good talking to you. See you later."

Tom watched her go, then sighed and wandered upstairs. Tattoo had finally arrived, and was in the kitchen with Shirleen, leaning against a counter. He motioned Tom over.

"Whatdya say?" The smell of beer came from his mouth in thick waves. Red veins spoiled his eyes, and he seemed shaky.

"It's good to see you, Tattoo. Have you recovered from the caves?"

"Never . . . go . . . again."

Shirleen laughed, and hugged him. "It was brave of my man to go in those awful caves."

"Don't . . . call me . . . your man."

"Sorry." Shirleen winked at Tom. "I forgot we're in public."

Tom smiled at them. "I guess I'll go back downstairs, and watch the dancing."

"I'll go with you," Shirleen said. "I want to be sure my guests are having fun."

But this was the wrong time for Shirleen to go downstairs. As she and Tom walked along the dim basement hallway, they saw two figures huddled together in the darkness with their arms wrapped tightly around each other. Startled, the pair separated, and Tom recognized Brandi. Beside her was the flashy man she'd been dancing with.

Shirleen gasped. "Brandi? What are you doing?"

"Nothing."

"Don't lie to me." She took a step toward the man, raising her hand. "My daughter's too young for you. Get out of this house."

The man mumbled something, then squeezed around Shirleen and hurried up the stairs. Brandi looked at her mother defiantly. "Leave me alone. I can make my own decisions."

"You're still an immature child, Brandi. You just proved that."

"It's my life!"

"Not while you're still under my roof."

"Then maybe I'll move out!"

Brandi shoved past Tom and raced for the stairs. For a moment Shirleen stared after her, then she also made for the stairs. Tom leaned against the wall, feeling rotten about what had happened.

Then he ran upstairs, found Shirleen sobbing in the kitchen, and managed to learn from Tattoo that Brandi had taken off from the house.

Rushing outside, Tom looked up and down the road. Nothing moved except dark leaves which trembled under a street light, and a cat which leapt to the top of a fence. It paused to gaze at Tom, then disappeared into the night.

From close by came the sound of highway traffic. Tom ran toward it, and saw Brandi on the roadside. Headlights lit her face as cars passed, ignoring her outstretched thumb.

"Brandi," Tom said, as he approached, "I'm sorry about what happened."

"Forget it, Tom. Just leave me alone."

"Aren't you coming back to the house?"

"No! I'm sick of that woman, and her fat boyfriend."

"What about Great Granny? She'll be really upset."

Doubt crossed Brandi's face. For a moment she lowered her thumb, then shook her head. "Great Granny will have to survive on her own."

"Come on back, Brandi. Please."

"Beat it, Tom. I'm on my own now, and it's for good."

Tom stared at her, trying to think of the right words to use. A car slowed as the driver examined Brandi, then the man saw Tom standing nearby and drove on. Someone yelled from a pickup heading in the other direction, and another man seemed ready to stop until he noticed Tom.

"Brandi, do you remember what you said at the hockey game?"

She shook her head.

"If you get in a guy's car, and he wants to kill you, there's no escape."

Her thumb wavered.

"You said that, Brandi! Don't you believe it?"

Brandi put both arms around her body, and hugged herself. "It's so cold out here. I'm freezing."

"That's because you're scared, Brandi. Don't hitch. Please!"

"I'm not scared of anything!" Her hand flashed out, and she stepped into the road to be more easily seen by drivers. "Get out of here, Tom."

Suddenly furious at her attitude, Tom walked swiftly away. Somehow he hoped that she would call his name, and return with him to the house, but he heard nothing until there was the sudden screech of brakes.

Turning, Tom saw that a big white car had stopped for Brandi. She got inside, smiling at the dark shape of the driver, then the car pulled away and disappeared into the night. Tom managed to see a jumble of letters on the license plate, but he was too far away to read them. Feeling very worried for Brandi, he walked quickly home.

The party was definitely over. The last of the guests were leaving; inside, the residents of *Shirleen's Place* sat in the living room, their faces mournful. When Tom entered the room, Shirleen looked up hopefully.

"Is she with you?"

"No."

She wiped at her red eyes. "I should never have fought with her."

Great Granny shook her head. "Brandi's your daughter. You must have standards for her behaviour, or she won't respect you."

The Maestro nodded. "Absolutely correct."

Tattoo looked a lot more sober, but his words were still thick on his tongue. "She'll be back soon. Just wandering around. Got a temper, that girl."

Shirleen nodded. "Yes, you're right. She's just out, walking around the neighbourhood."

Tom had been dreading this moment. With a rapidly beating heart, he told Shirleen about seeing Brandi hitch a ride. The room was terribly quiet while he spoke, then Tattoo lurched to his feet.

"I'll find Brandi. Bring her back." He stumbled to the hallway, pulled some keys out of a jacket pocket, and turned to Tom. "You come along. Show me the direction she went."

Tom looked at the Maestro. "Is it okay?"

"Just go to the highway, Tom, so Tattoo knows which way the car took Brandi. Then walk home."

Dietmar stood up. "I'll go, too."

A few minutes later, Tattoo's car turned onto the highway. Tom pointed out where Brandi had stood, and the direction the white car had gone, then reached for the door handle. But Tattoo put his foot to the floor, and the car rushed on into the night.

"Stay with me, Tom. May need your eyes. Can't see so good tonight."

Tom held on tight as Tattoo kept his foot pressed hard on the accelerator. They roared onto the orange bridge, crossed the double line to pass a slow-moving truck, then burned around a corner on the far side of the road. An A&W sign rose up ahead, then flashed past the window and was left behind. Darkness swallowed the car.

"Slow down, Tattoo," Tom said nervously. "This is such a twisty road."

"Gotta find her. Can't waste time."

"You're going to kill us."

Headlights came at them out of nowhere. Tattoo veered, tires screamed, and an angry horn died away into the night. "Wrong side of the road," Tattoo mumbled, wiping at his eyes. "Where's that white car?"

"Please stop, Tattoo. Let me out."

For the first time, Dietmar spoke. "Relax, Austen. Tattoo knows this road like the back of his hand."

"Yeah," Tattoo muttered. "Back my hand."

His bloodshot eyes gleamed in the glow of lights from the dashboard. The dim shape of trees rushed past the windows, and still he kept his foot pressed to the floor.

"Please, Tattoo!"

"Gotta find Brandi. Need your help."

"That's right," Dietmar said. "Don't you care about finding Brandi?"

Finally Tom acted. Leaning forward, he put a finger down his throat. His stomach heaved, and he gagged and retched. As vomit rose in his throat, Tattoo slammed on the brakes.

"Stop that! My car will stink!"

They pulled over. Tom reached for the handle, and got quickly out.

"Come on, Austen," Dietmar said, "don't be a wimp. Stay with us."

"Forget it, Oban. My life's important to me. It's the only one I've got."

Tattoo leaned toward Tom, his eyes angry. "Get back inside. I order you."

With a shaking hand, Tom closed the door and

stepped back from the car. Moments later, he was standing alone in the night.

8

The next morning, Brandi was still gone.

Tom had reached home after a long walk, and eventually Tattoo rolled in with Dietmar, but through the long night no word came from Brandi. The police were on the alert, but there was little they could do since Brandi had made her own decision to leave home.

"We've got to *act*," Tattoo exclaimed. "I'm going crazy, just sitting here."

Slamming down his coffee mug, he started pacing

the living room. Great Granny watched him, her eyes watery and red from weeping, while Shirleen stood motionless at the window. In her hands was a framed picture of Brandi.

"She's gone forever." Shirleen's voice was only a whisper. "Why didn't I ever say I love her?"

"She knew that, Shirleen."

"I never told her. I thought there was plenty of time."

Tattoo ran a hand over the black stubble on his face. "If that kidnapper's got Brandi, he must be holding her with the other kids. They can't be in a house because a neighbour would have become suspicious by now, so where are they?"

"Maybe he's built a cabin in the forest," Tom suggested.

Tattoo shook his head. "The police air patrols would have spotted a new cabin, and checked it out."

"Perhaps he fixed up an old place."

Tattoo stared at Tom. Then he took a couple of giant strides across the room, seized Tom's shoulders, and gripped them in powerful hands. "That's it! That's got to be the answer!" Swinging around, he faced the others. "This kid is brilliant!"

Tom wriggled free. "What did I do?"

Tattoo slapped his big hands together. "I know where he's got the kids! Remember I told you about those old mine buildings, up near Cody Caves? I figured somebody was planning to live there, but I bet that kidnapper was fixing them up. He's holding the kids there!"

"Why keep them at an old mine?"

Tattoo shrugged. "Who knows? The guy's a kook, so

anything's possible. Maybe he's like those people you talked about, the ones who steal replacement babies."

"Are you going to phone the police?"

"Not with the reputation I've got with the cops. I'll have to check on my own." He grabbed Shirleen. "Put down that picture, and come with me. You should get out of this house."

Pulling loose, Shirleen faced him angrily. "Stop running my life."

"I'm not."

"You're always ordering me around, but now it's over. We're finished, Tattoo."

"Relax, Shirleen. Come with me, and you'll soon feel better."

"I'm not going anywhere."

A look of terrible sadness passed over Tattoo's face, then it was replaced by an angry frown. "Okay, I'll go alone."

"I'd like to help," Tom said.

"Sure, if you want."

Nothing more was said by Shirleen, who studied Brandi's picture before returning to her place at the window. Great Granny wished them luck, and so did the Maestro. Dietmar was still asleep in bed.

Soon after, they were driving along the North Shore Road. Tattoo was absolutely silent. His eyes were grim and his knuckles were white on the wheel. Tom said nothing, knowing Tattoo was thinking about his argument with Shirleen.

North of Balfour, all signs of civilization were left behind as they travelled through thick forest and then reached a rugged area where signs warned about the danger of slides, the road twisted dangerously around sheer cliffs, and the pavement had been scarred and pitted by rocks which had crashed down from above. As Tattoo swerved to avoid a boulder in the middle of the road, the driver of a southbound camper waved a friendly greeting but was ignored. The silence continued until they were past Ainsworth.

"This is it," Tattoo said, pulling into a dirt road and stopping the car.

"But we aren't at Cody Caves."

"I know that," Tattoo snapped. "I'm not a fool. We walk from here."

"But ..."

"My car could never make it up that road to Cody Caves. Besides, this way is a shortcut. Don't you trust me?"

They started walking up a hill. The forest closed around them.

"You know something, Tom? I admire you for getting out of my car last night. I was too drunk to be driving. That took real guts."

"Thanks, Tattoo."

"I've never had much courage. That's one of my many problems. If I wasn't around, Shirleen would get on better with Brandi. But where can I go? I've got no job, no training. A person can't get hired these days without a skill to offer a boss. I was a fool to drop out of school, but I've always been a fool."

For the first time, Tom noticed that the dirt road through the forest was like the place where Simon had been attacked. Where was that man now? Had he been the kidnapper, or someone else?

"Ever seen one of those?" Tattoo pointed at a

hornet's nest. "You know those are grey? The hornets take wood from weathered buildings and chew it into paper to make their nests." He sighed. "I used to love teaching my son about the forest."

"Is he dead?"

"No, but he might as well be."

"Why?"

"I'm a loser. If my boy was here, he wouldn't love me. His mind is poisoned against me."

"But, if you haven't seen your son for a long time, how can you know that his mind's poisoned against you?"

Tattoo looked carefully at Tom, and then almost smiled. "You know, I never thought of that."

"Maybe you could find him."

"Forget it," Tattoo said angrily. "There are no happy endings in my life."

They walked on in silence. Even though the forest was cool, sweat ran in long trickles down Tom's back, and he began to wonder if they would ever reach their goal. It was hard work climbing over the many fallen trees which littered the dirt road.

"Are we almost there?"

Tattoo sat down abruptly on a log. "What if I'm wrong about the mine building, Tom? Everyone is counting on me to find Brandi. I love her like a daughter, but we're always fighting. She'd be happier with me gone." He looked at the forest. "You can tell that's a cedar, because the bark pulls away in long strips. Cedars rot from the inside. Did you know that?"

"No. How'd you find out?"

"I could tell you plenty about the forest. The air we're breathing is full of invisible spoors which will become fungus on trees, or turn into the lichen which Indians used as emergency food. The yew has a bright red berry with poisonous seeds. If you needed to, you could survive in the forest on the berries by spitting out the seeds."

"How come you know so much?"

"I love the forest. I'm at peace here." Tattoo peeled spongy moss away from a boulder. "I've always been a dreamer, longing for the good life but never willing to work for it. Now look at the mess I'm in! I wanted to be a biker, but I only went to biker movies. I wanted to be a great rock star like Jerry Lee Lewis, but I never got further than buying his records. What a wasted life!"

Tattoo seemed overwhelmed by emotion. "I've ruined my life! Every opportunity wasted. Why can't I be the Killer? Because I haven't got the guts."

The killer?

Suddenly, everything made sense to Tom.

He backed away from Tattoo, then turned and ran. Down the dirt road he flew, leaping over fallen trees and pushing past low bushes, until he reached the highway. Still he ran, searching for a place to wait safely for a passing car. Somehow he had to reach a town, and alert the police about Tattoo's guilt.

It was terrible to think about, yet the evidence was all there. Tom stopped running and stared at the lake, wishing he still trusted Tattoo. In the water, a few rotting pilings were held together by long-rusted cables, the only remains of a pier where paddle-wheelers had once collected ore from the mines. If Tattoo had got him to the mine buildings, what would he have done?

Tom shivered. He heard a car approaching, but

sheltered behind a boulder until the last second in case it was Tattoo. When the car came into sight he waved his arms, but rushed past without stopping.

A dead butterfly was moving in the dirt at the side of the road. Bending down, Tom saw it was being dragged home by a tiny ant. As he watched the ant haul its burden over rocks that must have seemed like mountains, another vehicle approached. Tom was thrilled to see that the driver was Kendall Steele. The 4x4 stopped, and Tom ran to get inside.

"I must get to the police right away, Mr. Steele. Tattoo is the kidnapper, and I know where he's got the children."

"Slow down," Kendall Steele said, raising a hand. His blue eyes studied Tom. "Who are you?"

"Tom Austen. You took me into Cody Caves."

Kendall Steele reached into the back seat for a couple of soft drinks and handed one to Tom. Then he looked out at the wide waters of the lake. "I've missed the children a lot, son. But everything's fine now."

The drink tasted odd, but Tom was so hot and sweaty that he didn't care. "Tattoo's broke, so he turned to kidnapping for money. But he didn't have the courage to send out ransom notes, so now he's working up the nerve to finish off the kids. He said he hasn't got the guts to be a killer, but he may change his mind now that I know the truth. We've got to rescue them!"

"It was such a terrible accident. The other driver had bald tires on his car. I'll never forgive him for that."

There was a loud crash from outside the 4x4. Tom saw that a cluster of rocks had crashed down the cliff face, leaving behind a cloud of red dust. It hung in the air, then drifted slowly away across the highway.

"Shouldn't we get going?"

"Finish your drink," Kendall Steele said, lighting a cigarette.

"I have." Tom put the empty bottle in the back seat. "We'd better phone the police from Ainsworth."

Kendall Steele put the 4x4 in gear. Tom expected him to turn around and make for Ainsworth, but instead the man continued north. "Are we going to Kaslo? That's a long way from here."

There was no reply. Kendall Steele turned to Tom, but his eyes seemed to look through him. Then he smiled. "Have a drink."

"I already did."

Tom's face felt strange. He lifted a numb hand to touch the skin. It felt like rubber. His tongue seemed to have grown larger inside his mouth. As he shook his head, trying to clear it of fog, he realized they had left the highway and were climbing the gravel road toward Cody Caves.

"This . . ."

The rest of the words wouldn't come. The 4x4 roared and growled as it raced through a huge puddle, spraying water over the windshield. The junk on the floor bounced around, and Tom kicked aside a scuffed cowboy boot that got under his feet. They passed an old log house which had collapsed into ruins at the side of the road.

"I wanna give you some good news," Kendall Steele said. "Now you belong to my family. You'll be outta the rat race, and you'll be my son."

Wanna. Outta. The fake security guard had used

those words. As Tom's confused mind tried to process this information, he saw the cigarette in Kendall Steele's hand and remembered the security guard smoking.

That scuffed cowboy boot. Tom looked at it on the floor, feeling nauseated. Images ran through his mind of Simon in the woods, being choked by a man who wore scuffed cowboy boots.

"I want . . ." Tom's mouth felt frozen, useless. "Get . . . out."

"Don't you feel well?"

Tom shook his head.

"These will pep you up." Kendall Steele held out three green pills. "Just swallow them, and you'll feel good."

Tom remembered a girl named Brandi. She'd talked about a man who gave kids doped pop, and capsules he called pep pills. But Brandi said they were really knock-out drops. "Brandi . . . said . . . no."

"Go on, have them. You'll get a real lift."

"O . . . kay." Tom took the pills, and raised them to his mouth with a shaking hand. As he swallowed, the 4x4 passed a sign reading *Cody Caves* and continued deeper into the forest. Beside the road, a cold white stream boiled down among boulders.

"Here we are." The 4x4 braked to a stop. "I'll help you walk."

Kendall Steele walked around to open the passenger door. As he did, Tom dropped the green pills from his hand, where they'd been hidden, and kicked them under the seat. He had to pretend to be heavily drugged by the pills until he could think of a means to get away.

The forest seemed to be a solid wall of greens, all blurred together, but Kendall Steele forced a route through it, holding Tom with his strong hand. Somehow, Tom knew, he had to escape in the next few minutes. But how? He forced his mind to think despite the fog which overwhelmed it. Once his father had shown how he couldn't lift Tom and carry him across a room. *Remember, Tom, a limp body is impossible to carry.* Sun struck his face, and he saw they'd entered a clearing. Nearby stood three old buildings, faded with age. In the face of the nearby mountainside was the tumble-down opening to a mine shaft.

"I'm . . . sick." Tom flopped to the ground.

"Get up." Kendall Steele prodded Tom with his foot. "I want you to come inside to join your brother and sister."

Tom groaned. ". . . sick."

Kendall Steele put his arms under Tom. He struggled to lift his limp body, but the dead weight was too much for him. The man stood over Tom for a moment, then turned away.

He hurried up the steps of the nearest building, unlocked the door, and went inside. The moment the door closed, Tom got to his feet and staggered toward the forest. His body seemed terribly heavy, and he felt as if he was wading through molasses as he lurched forward.

"Hey!"

Kendall Steele stood by the door, staring at Tom. As he came down the steps, Tom changed direction and made for the entrance to the mine. His feet stumbled over the rusty rails and wooden ties of an abandoned mine railway, and then he was inside.

Water dripped somewhere, and Tom suddenly had a horrifying vision of rats attacking. He looked toward the daylight at the entrance to the mine, wishing he could return that way, then staggered deeper along the shaft. He must find a hiding place.

The air smelled of dirt and water and metal. His foot kicked a rock and it bounced away, the sound echoing throughout the mine shaft. Tom paused, listening for Kendall Steele, then went further.

Was that a noise? He turned, expecting to see the daylight, but now there was only darkness everywhere. A moan escaped from his lips. He put out a hand, touched a rocky wall, and slumped down.

A long time passed before Tom heard another noise, which sounded like something breathing. He tried not to think of the rats, and hugged his body against the cold. Yes! He'd been right, there *was* something breathing. A wave of terrible fear swept through Tom. His eyes stared at the black air.

A scraping sound came to him, then the sudden flare of light. Close by, around a corner, a cigarette lighter had sprung to life. Tom huddled back against the wall, watching the light glint from the wet walls of the mine as cautious footsteps approached. They reached the corner, rounded it, and came closer.

At the last second Tom sprang from hiding, ready to fight his way free. But a familiar voice shouted in surprise, and Tom recognized the face of the man who held the flickering yellow light. It was Tattoo.

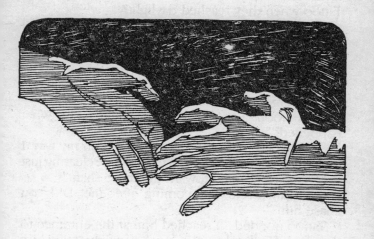

9

The lighter went out, and fear of Tattoo leapt inside Tom. "I surrender! I won't fight, just don't let it be dark."

The yellow light flared, showing Tattoo's face. He was smiling. "Surrender? What do you mean?"

"I know you're partners with Kendall Steele."

Tattoo laughed. The sound echoed inside the mine shaft. "You'd better come with me."

They walked together toward the exit from the mine. Tom's mind was no longer foggy, but he remained deeply worried. How could he escape from Tattoo when they reached daylight?

But escape wasn't necessary. When they stepped into sunshine, Tom saw Kendall Steele on the steps of the mine building. His hands and feet were bound with rope, and he had also been tied to the porch. The man was staring at the ground, and said nothing as they emerged from the mine.

Tom looked at Tattoo in surprise. "What happened?"

"After you ran from me, I continued on my way. I had to know about the kids. I reached the clearing just as you were running toward the mine shaft."

"Kendall Steele was coming after me. Did you chase him?"

Tattoo nodded. "I reached him at the entrance to the mine. He didn't put up much of a fight. I tied him up, then went inside the building to release the kids."

"Then you were right! The kids were held prisoner here."

"Except for Brandi." Tattoo took a deep breath. "I couldn't find her, Tom. I searched all three buildings before I went into the mine for you."

"Where'd you get the cigarette lighter?"

"From Kendall Steele's pocket."

Tom looked toward the nearest building. Chuck Cohen stood in the doorway, hands in the pockets of dirty jeans. His face looked pale, but he seemed to recognize Tom. With a faint smile on his lips, he came slowly down the steps and crossed the clearing.

"Hi Chuck," Tom said. "Do you remember me?"

He nodded. "Are we going home now?"

"You bet! Where's Tippi?"

Chuck pointed toward the forest. "She was scared, and took off running in that direction. I couldn't stop her."

Tattoo swore. "How long's she been gone?"

"A few minutes."

"You'd better stay here, Tom. Don't worry about Kendall Steele. He can't get loose from those ropes."

"I'd rather help you find Tippi."

"Okay. Let's not waste time arguing." Tattoo looked at Chuck. "Wait right here, sonny. We'll get Tippi, then take you home."

They followed a path which led along the face of the mountain into the forest. It was dark, except for one small clearing where the sun reached down to touch the white bark of a stand of poplars. Birds sang in the trees, then fell silent when Tattoo called Tippi's name. There was no reply.

"Poor Kendall Steele," Tattoo said. "I remember Shirleen telling me about him losing his kids in a car accident, but you wouldn't believe he'd steal a new family."

"You think that's what happened?"

"Looks like it. He'd fixed up the mine building like a proper house, complete with a TV set. But there was no electricity, and the doors had locks to keep the kids prisoner. How pathetic." Tattoo called Tippi's name, but the forest remained silent. "I've lost my family, too, but at least they're alive. With luck I could start over with my kids, but Kendall Steele never had that chance."

"Listen!"

Sounds came from somewhere ahead. They shouted Tippi's name, then ran forward. When they finally saw her, she was standing at a rocky cleft in the hillside. Her frightened face looked in their direction, then she disappeared from sight.

"That's Cody Caves!" Tattoo said. "Why's she gone in there?"

"She must be scared of us. Maybe she thinks we're going to lock her up again."

"That's nuts. I just set her free."

"We'd better get her out, Tattoo."

He stared at the rocky opening. "I said I'd never go back in there. But if we wait for help to come she'll be lost."

"And there's hypothermia. She's only wearing a dress."

Tattoo swore again. "Why do these things happen to me?"

"Wait here, and I'll go after her."

"No way." Tattoo held up the cigarette lighter. "This is our only light, and there's no hard hats. George Harshbarger wouldn't approve."

"We'd better get moving."

Tom slid through the opening, and darkness closed around him. He shivered in his thin shirt as he breathed the cold, damp air. Tattoo squeezed through the cleft, then flicked on the lighter. The feeble glare showed little more than their faces.

From somewhere came the eerie sound of sobbing. For a moment it stopped, then echoed around them again.

"Listen to me, Tippi." Tattoo tried to sound gentle, but his deep voice seemed harsh in the darkness. "We want to help you. Please come here."

Rocks clattered. The sobbing grew fainter, then died away.

"I think she's crawled along that passage," Tom said, "the one leading to the other caves."

"Let's get her."

Slowly they edged forward, reaching carefully with their feet to find the way. Tom remembered the hibernating spiders, and pictured them dropping into his hair.

"This is frightening."

Tattoo grunted. "You're so right."

A rocky wall appeared ahead. Tattoo moved the lighter back and forth until he spotted the narrow passage. "I'll go first," he said, kneeling down. As he crawled inside, his body hid the light. Black air suffocated Tom.

He knelt down, and slithered into the passage. He could feel mud under his hands, and very quickly his clothes became soaked. He kept his head low, knowing that jagged rocks were just above. The darkness was terrible.

"You okay?" Tattoo waited at the end of the passage, holding the lighter. His body was covered with mud, and he was already shaking from the cold. "We've got to find her soon. The lighter won't last forever."

Tom hadn't thought of that. He stared at the tiny yellow flame, knowing it was their only link to safety. "Don't let water drip on it."

"Where is she?" Tattoo faced the darkness. "It's worse than a dungeon in here. It's more like an underground tomb."

"Don't say that. I'm scared enough."

From nearby came two sounds. One was the stream, rushing unseen through the cavern, and the other was Tippi's sobbing. It was muffled, but they knew she was close.

This time Tattoo didn't scare the girl by calling to her. Instead he moved slowly toward the sound of her sobbing, and finally stopped at the base of a tiny passage. "She's crawled up this chimney," he whispered to Tom. "I'll have to go after her, and talk her out."

"You're too big to fit into this chimney." Tom knelt at the opening. "Give me the lighter."

"Be careful it doesn't get snuffed out by the mud."

Tom nodded. He looked at the chimney, memorizing its shape, then flicked off the lighter. Darkness consumed him, sudden and overwhelming. Fighting to keep calm, he reached to find the walls of the chimney and slithered inside.

Panic rose in his throat. For a moment he was convinced he couldn't do it, and they'd have to leave Tippi until help came. But cold was working steadily deeper into his flesh, and he knew little time was left.

He started forward, then his head struck rock. The pain made him cry out. He lowered his face closer to the mud and worked his way forward on his elbows and knees.

Tippi sobbed somewhere in the darkness, then was silent.

"I'm a friend," Tom said gently. "You must let me help."

No reply. Tom moved forward again, then listened. He could hear the girl's breathing, and the wet sound of her weeping. He reached into the pocket, found the lighter, and took it out. Praying it would work, he flicked it with muddy fingers. Nothing. Again he tried, and light filled the passage.

Tippi's face was straight ahead. Somehow she had

got twisted around inside the chimney, and was looking straight at Tom. The yellow light reflected from her frightened eyes; filthy hair hung in black strands to her shoulders.

"We're your friends, Tippi. We want to take you home, to see your Mommy and Daddy." Tom reached to her. "Take my hand. Please."

For long moments nothing happened. Then Tippi's hand came slowly forward, and Tom felt the touch of her cold fingers. He smiled. "I'll back up slowly, and you come with me."

As he moved back he released Tippi's hand, but she whimpered and quickly he reached for her again. Then, very slowly and very carefully, struggling to protect the lighter from the mud, he led her down the long chimney until at last he felt Tattoo's strong hands seize his body and help him to stand.

Tattoo held the lighter while Tom continued talking soothingly to Tippi. She got to her feet and then huddled against his body, frightened of Tattoo. But he seemed to understand why she would be afraid after being a prisoner; ignoring her fear, he led the way to the outer cavern.

Brilliant blue sunshine spilled from the cleft in the rocks. Joy filled Tom. At last it was all over. Except for Brandi . . . where was she?

The safe return of the children threw Nelson into an uproar. The media swept down on *Shirleen's Place*, seeking details and interviews, but Tattoo did everything possible to avoid the role of hero.

He failed, however, and his picture was seen everywhere. This resulted in two welcome events. The first was the return of Brandi, who walked in the door to a jubilant reunion with her mother and Great Granny.

"I hitched a ride with that hockey coach, Burton Donco," she explained. "He was just driving around, trying to cool off about his team losing, so he gave me a lift to Kaslo." She shook her head, smiling. "I spent two days hanging around, thinking how much I love my family. Then the kids were found, and I saw you on TV. I felt so lonely! A really nice Mountie drove me home after I went to them for help."

The second happy result of the publicity came only hours later. As everyone sat around the table, eating a meal, they heard the doorbell. "Not another reporter!" groaned Tattoo, going to answer the door.

But no member of the media stood on the porch. Instead it was Simon. He smiled shyly, and held out his hand to Tattoo. "Hello, Dad. It's good to see you again."

Tattoo put his arms around Simon, and hugged him tightly. "I've missed you so much, son."

Tom stared at them in shock, then his eyes went to Shirleen. She was obviously as surprised as the others, but then she smiled. "Invite your boy inside, Tattoo. Maybe he'll have some food."

Simon came into the room with his arm around Tattoo's shoulders. "No thanks, Shirleen. I'm too excited to eat."

Tattoo hugged Simon again. "I've been scared of this moment, but I feel great now that it's happened."

The Maestro looked at him. "Won't you explain?"

"Sure thing," Tattoo said. "I'd lost track of my boy and his mother. Then that day at the logger sports events I spotted Simon. I realized he was here for the hockey tournament, so I did my best to avoid him."

"Why?"

Tattoo shrugged. "I thought he was poisoned against me. Tom changed my mind on that, but I still didn't want to ruin Simon's life."

"That was crazy, Dad." Simon grinned. "When I saw you on TV, I was so excited. But I had to work up the nerve to see you again."

"Folks say you're quite the hockey player. I tried to ignore that, because I wasn't able to share your success."

"I'd like you to watch me play, Dad."

"It's too late. The tournament's over."

"There's always next winter, in Tumbler Ridge. We'll have plenty of games."

"Yeah, well, maybe I'll get up there for one."

Simon shook his head. "No, Dad. I want you to come back with me, and get a job in Tumbler Ridge. There's plenty of work."

Tom glanced at Shirleen. To his surprise, she looked pleased at the idea. "Go for it, Tattoo," she said. "You always talked about getting a second chance. Here it is."

"Maybe I will." Tattoo sat down at the table. "You know, I keep thinking about that poor Kendall Steele trying to rebuild his family. I've got an opportunity that he never had."

Tom looked at him. "Now that Simon's here to protect me, I'll make a confession. I thought you'd kidnapped the kids, and were about to finish them off."

"That's why you ran from me?"

"Sure, but you scared me. You said you didn't have the courage to be the killer."

"So that's it!" Tattoo burst out laughing, then went to the living room and returned with a Jerry Lee Lewis record called *The Killer Rocks On.* "You know," he said, grinning, "I've always regretted not having the guts to work hard at becoming a great star like Jerry Lee Lewis, whose nickname is the Killer."

Everyone joined in his laughter, including Tom. Then he turned to Dietmar. "Don't say it! The great detective bombs again."

"Right on, Austen! I wouldn't even hire you to find the end of a stick."

"Well, I *almost* worked this one out. I just missed a couple of clues, like at the Big Tee when Kendall Steele knew about the kidnapper's fake security guard uniform and gold badge, even though the police hadn't released those details to the public."

"I noticed that, but didn't say anything."

"Sure you did, Oban," Tom said with heavy sarcasm. "Anyway, I also heard Kendall Steele say wanna and outta, but I'd forgotten the kidnapper used those words. And he smoked, and had a deep voice. I learned Kendall Steele didn't have a family but later, during the Cody expedition, he talked about how his son would experience the caves. On that trip I even saw the scuffed cowboy boots the kidnapper had worn both at the mall and when he attacked Simon."

"So," Simon said, "that really was Kendall Steele?"

Tom nodded. "Maybe he saw us sitting on the lakeshore and thought we were young kids, then he realized his mistake and panicked."

The Maestro sighed. "That unfortunate man seems to have been a schizophrenic. At times he must have been completely out of touch with reality, living his role as father of the children at the mine building, and other times he'd be perfectly normal. It's a sad case."

"So is Austen," Dietmar said. "The kids back home will love hearing the story of how he blew this one."

"You're right," Tom said. "Maybe I should change my mind, and consider a future as a chef." He looked toward the stove. "Do you think my soup's ready yet, Shirleen?"

"Sure, Tom, but you've waited too long to serve it. Nobody's hungry now. It's a shame, after all the work you did."

"I'll eat your soup," Dietmar said. "No sense letting it go to waste."

"Great, Dietmar. I was counting on the Human Garborator to come through." Tom poured a bowl of steaming soup. "Enjoy, enjoy."

"I've never seen grey soup before." Dietmar lifted a spoonful, blew on it, and tried some. "Not bad! Congratulations, Austen."

"Thank you."

Very quickly Dietmar polished off the soup, then helped himself to a second bowl. As he worked his way through it, Tom watched him with an unusual smile. Then he turned to the others. "Since George Harshbarger isn't here to object, maybe we can talk about world records. What's the largest meat dish eaten by people?"

No answer.

"Roast camel. It's served at some Bedouin wedding feasts. They put eggs into a fish, which goes inside a chicken, then the chicken is stuffed into a roast sheep, which is put inside the camel before it is cooked and served."

"Amazing!" Great Granny exclaimed.

"Now, what's the world's most unusual food?" Tom waited for a reply, then smiled. "In Korea, earthworm soup is considered a delicacy. People there love it. I thought you might, too."

"Very interesting," the Maestro said. He jotted the information in his notebook, then suddenly looked at the grey soup in Dietmar's bowl. "You don't mean ...? Surely you can't have ..."

Tom shrugged. "If I'm going to be a chef, I should serve international dishes. Making earthworm soup sounded like an interesting challenge."

Dietmar gazed at his bowl in horror, then stared at Tom with bulging eyes. Clutching his mouth, he stumbled from the table and raced for the bathroom. The door slammed.

"What's wrong with him?" Tom asked innocently.

He went to the stove, poured out a bowl of the grey soup, and returned to the table. Lifting a spoonful to his mouth, he looked around the table. "Isn't anyone else hungry?"

"Forget it!" Tattoo said. "How can you eat that stuff?"

"But it's delicious." Tom ate some, smacking his lips with pleasure. "I don't think earthworms would taste very good, but this is certainly the best mushroom soup I ever tasted."

As everyone laughed, Tom listened to the anguished sounds coming from the bathroom. "You know," he said, smiling happily, "Dietmar wanted the kids back home to hear a good story. Maybe they'll enjoy this one."

Have you joined

THE ERIC WILSON MYSTERY CLUB

?????

It's exciting, and it's all FREE!

Here's what you'll receive:
— a membership card
— a regular newsletter
— a chance to win books personally
  autographed to you by Eric Wilson

It's FREE, so just send your name, age,
address and postal code to:

The Eric Wilson Mystery Club
Collins Publishers
100 Lesmill Road
Don Mills, Ontario
M3B 2T5

About the Author

Eric Wilson was born in Ottawa and now lives in British Columbia. He is often "on the road" visiting schools to speak about his writing, or exploring various regions of Canada to discover settings for future books.

His earlier mysteries are described on the following pages, and you can also learn how to get your membership in the exciting Eric Wilson Mystery Club.

MURDER
ON *THE CANADIAN*
A Tom Austen Mystery
Eric Wilson

*As the train's whistle moaned out of the black night,
Tom fell into an unhappy sleep. It was broken by a
scream.*

The agonizing sound of a woman's scream hurls
Tom Austen into the middle of a murder plot on
board the sleek passenger train, *The Canadian*.
Who is responsible for the death of lovely Catherine
Saks? As Tom investigates the strange collection of
travellers who share Car 165, he gets closer and
closer to the truth . . . and then, without warning, he
is suddenly face-to-face with the killer, and his own
life is threatened in the most alarming possible way.

*"In MURDER ON THE CANADIAN there is
excitement from the start; the first dozen pages
produce a bomb, a "deadly enemy", a drunk and a
beautiful woman . . . there are plenty of suspects to
lay false trails, and the action moves as fast as the
train."*
Times Literary Supplement

VANCOUVER NIGHTMARE
A Tom Austen Mystery
Eric Wilson

Tom's body was shaking. Spider could return at any moment, and there was still a closet to search. Was it worth the risk? He hesitated, picturing Spider bursting through the door with rage on his face.

A chance meeting with a drug pusher named Spider takes Tom Austen into the grim streets of Vancouver's Skid Road, where he poses as a runaway while searching for information to help the police smash a gang which is cynically hooking young kids on drugs.

Suddenly unmasked as a police agent, Tom is trapped in the nightmarish underworld of Vancouver as the gang closes in, determined to get rid of the young meddler at any cost.

" 'The coffin was open, the air black and musty all around.' Who could resist a mystery begun in such a fashion? This fast-paced tale of drug smuggling and deceit will be an instant success..."
Canadian Book Review Annual

DISNEYLAND HOSTAGE
A Liz Austen Mystery
Eric Wilson

Renfield held a wriggling, hairy tarantula in his hand. Suddenly the maniac cackled, and ran straight at me with the giant spider!

Facing a tarantula is just one of the exciting, suspenseful moments that Liz Austen experiences in DISNEYLAND HOSTAGE. On her own during a California holiday, unable to seek the help of her brother Tom, she is plunged into the middle of an international plot when a boy named Ramón disappears from his room at the Disneyland Hotel. Has Ramón been taken hostage? Before Liz can answer that question, her own safety is threatened when terrorists strike at the most unlikely possible target: Disneyland itself.

"He recreates in rich detail the wonders of Disneyland... The plot moves quickly to an unpredictable climax, taking clever twists along the way."
Quill & Quire, Toronto

THE GHOST OF LUNENBURG MANOR
A Tom & Liz Austen Mystery
Eric Wilson
"Would you like to visit a haunted house?"

With this invitation from a man named Professor
Zinck, Tom Austen and his sister Liz are swept up
in spine-chilling events that will baffle you, and
grip you in suspense.

A fire burning on the sea . . . icy fingers in the
night . . . an Irish Setter that suddenly won't go near
its master's bedroom . . . a host of strange characters
with names like Black Dog, Henneyberry and
Roger Eliot-Stanton . . . these are the ingredients of
a mystery that challenges you to enter the ancient
hallways of Lunenburg Manor. . . *if you dare.*

*"Eric Wilson has once again produced an excellent,
fast-paced mystery. . . the richness of the Maritime
setting—replete with phantoms, folklore, stormy
seas and superstitions—enhances the story."*
The Ottawa Citizen

VAMPIRES OF OTTAWA

A Liz Austen Mystery

Eric Wilson

Suddenly the vampire rose up from behind a tombstone and fled, looking like an enormous bat with his black cape streaming behind in the moonlight.

Within the walls of a gloomy estate known as Blackwater, Liz Austen discovers the strange world of Baron Nicolai Zaba, a man who lives in constant fear. What is the secret of the ancient chapel's underground vault? Why are the words *In Evil Memory* scrawled on a wall? Who secretly threatens the Baron? All the answers lie within these pages but be warned: *reading this book will make your blood run cold.*

SUMMER OF DISCOVERY
Eric Wilson

Rico's teeth were chattering so loudly that everyone could hear. Ian's breath came in deep gasps. A gust of wind slammed through the old building, shaking it so hard that every shutter rattled, and then they heard the terrible sound. Somewhere upstairs, a voice was sobbing.

Do ghosts of hymn-singing children haunt a cluster of abandoned buildings on the Saskatchewan prairie? The story of how the kids from Terry Fox Cabin answer that question will thrill you from page one of this exciting book. Eric Wilson, author of many fast-moving mysteries, presents here a tale of adventure, humour and the triumph of the human spirit. It's an experience you'll never forget.